TRAITOR

BY

M G LESLIE

Copyright

Copyright © 2023 M G Leslie

The author, whom retains all rights to this book, also owns the email address below and may be contacted directly using that means of communication.

No part of this publication may be reproduced or stored in a retrieval system or transmitted in any form or by any means, electronic, mechanical, copying, recording or otherwise, without the author's written consent.

The author may be contacted via email at:

Mark.Leslie1966@gmail.com

This book may make reference to organisations and places. Whilst some of these representations may be correct, the author in no way guarantees that they are correct, as this book is a combination of publicly available information and the author's own ideas.

Any reference to third parties or organisations, under no circumstances represents an opinion or criticism in any way, whether positive or negative, about that party or organisation or its or their activities, actions, products, and/or views.

Preface

There are more Russian spies in Great Britain now than there were, even at the height of the Cold War. There are approximately six Russians spies for every British intelligence officer in the world.

They're mostly based in London and cities with a large Royal Navy presence.

Why do they follow the Royal Navy you may ask, as opposed to the Royal Air Force or the British Army?

The answer is an easy one - it's the nuclear missiles.

Britain is a nuclear power with an offensive capability that is entirely reliant on its nuclear submarines. A capability that Russian spies are tasked to gather intelligence on.

It goes without saying that, whilst their intelligence agencies adopt numerous traditional techniques to influence and exploit potential sources, they also have access to the latest technology.

They can send code and take remote control of mobile phones, listening in on conversations and reading texts.

Or they can just sit outside buildings and read the computer screen text and images by intercepting the electromagnetic radiation.

The longer it is displayed on your screen, the easier it is for them to read it.

And if that doesn't work, it's now possible to intercept

keystrokes from up to twenty-five metres away by capturing the electronic pulse the keys emit.

This may sound like the stuff of science fiction. It may sound like something you see in the movies - but it really isn't. This is reality - reality today!

It's a brutal world where the government sponsored agencies are no longer just interested in intelligence gathering and old-school espionage. These days, even the state-run agencies steal commercial secrets for financial gain.

Some even commit murder to silence their enemies. Although, that's nothing new.

This story follows the continuing adventures of Price, an ex-Paratrooper and now a member of a secret unit called The Increment, within the UK's Secret Intelligence Service - aka SIS or MI6 - or by its members, simply, The Firm.

In the prequel to this novel, **Killing The Killers**, the SIS Chief discovered Price had a secret relationship with a Chinese intelligence officer, Mary - a resourceful and ruthless spy who later also claimed to be covertly blackmailing and controlling a Russian agent named Alexei.

Ordinarily, Price and Alexei would expect to work for opposing intelligence services - in some ways akin to employees working for competing businesses.

However, during active service in Syria, face-to-face with members of the Islamic State (ISIS), they found themselves united against a common enemy, thereby establishing a bond that enabled them both to escape and live to fight another day.

Many months later though, something terrible would happen in London. Something that would begin a sequence of events and change their lives beyond all recognition.

Price and people like him are sometimes required to be ruthless - even brutal in the pursuit of their enemy.

We hope they're also loyal, despite operating in a secret world where lies and deceit are not just a matter of course, they're essential for survival.

The problem is, sometimes the line between good and bad can get a little blurred.

Sometimes, people lose all perspective and forget the difference between right and wrong.

Sometimes, there's even a traitor in the midst.

Chapters

Copyright	2
Preface	3
1. Angel	9
2. Innocent Victim?	16
3. The Courier	20
4. Let This Be A Lesson	33
5. Never Again	47
6. An Embittered End	55
7. Steak A Dozen Ways	58
8. Black Dolphin	69
9. Mary	73
10. Slavic Stepka	98
11. Waiting	121
12. Enemy By Association	132
13. Setting The Trap	153
14. On The Road	181
15. The Chase	208
16. The Traitor	237

1. Angel

It was just after midnight.

Mary stood next to her armour-plated Range Rover, watching as crates of AK47 rifles were carried from a sixty-year old Antanov AN-12 cargo plane to a dozen waiting trucks.

The Russian arms dealer stood next to her - checking them against the inventory Mary had provided.

As the last crate was loaded, he turned to face her and spoke, only for the second time since they had met - he was a man of few words.

"Fifty-thousand AK47 rifles and fifty-million rounds of ammunition."

Mary nodded, "As agreed."

The Russian man nodded back, reached in to his pocket and retrieved his mobile phone - tapping the screen a few times before looking back at Mary.

A few moments later, Mary's phone buzzed signifying that the financial transfer was complete.

"Nice doing business with you," the Russian added, as he turned and walked to the nearest truck.

Mary turned away and made eye contact with an imposing soldier, on the far side of the tarmac - armed to the teeth with RPG's and a floor mounted machine gun, just in case things didn't go quite to plan.

Mary indicated that they should get in the Range Rover. She had the money and it was time to go.

Slavic Stepka nodded back and, just as the trucks filed away down a dark track in to the woods, he packed up the weapons.

The Antanov, meanwhile, had made its way to the end of the makeshift runway - a kilometre-long strip of tarmac surrounded by the dense forest of the Rāzna National Park in the east of Latvia - not far from the Russian border.

Unbeknownst to Mary and everyone else, however, they were not alone. A figure, clad entirely in black so as to avoid being seen, had watched and recorded the meeting from the darkness of the woods.

Four hours later, Mary walked in to her hotel room in Latvia's capital, Riga.

She couldn't help smiling as she slipped off her shoes and prepared to take a shower.

She was wealthy beyond her wildest dreams. And perhaps as a result of her excitement, failed to remember the first rule when entering a room.

Check if someone is hiding in there!

Without so much as a second thought, she switched on the TV to check the latest news of the day. However, it wasn't the news that appeared on the screen. To her horror and surprise, it was her on the screen.

A video of her, the Russian arms dealer and the exchange.

Mary's heart skipped a beat as she reached for her gun.

But it wasn't to be.

A voice from the dark corner of the small room interrupted.

"I have a gun pointing directly at your head."

Mary spun around to face the person, having immediately recognised the voice.

It was a Russian agent, Alexei, who worked for her.

"Oh Mary. You think you're so good and yet you got sloppy. I've been following you for months.

I have so much evidence on you, documenting your illegal arms deals, I could have you locked away forever."

Mary slowly walked over to the door and switched on the main light for the room - before turning and staring directly back in to Alexei's eyes.

"Why don't you, then?" she asked, in a monotone, emotionless voice.

Alexei smiled, "Because it's time for some revenge. You're now working for me. Unless of course you want this video, and many more, to arrive in front of your superiors.

I'm sure they would be more than a little upset to hear that you've been secretly selling arms to their enemies."

"I'm sure your superiors would not be pleased when I tell them about your sexual fetishes. The kind of things you like are just as illegal in Russia as they are elsewhere," Mary retorted.

Alexei laughed, "They'd lock me up - that's for sure. But once your superiors know about you, I doubt you'd live long enough to see the inside of a prison. You and that sick bastard, Stepka. I guess you found out about him and his perversions which is why he's working for you?"

Mary nodded, "Yes."

"Well it's over. I'm in charge now."

Mary remained silent. She knew he had the upper hand for the moment. She also knew there was only one solution.

He had to die.

But now wasn't the time or the place. So, she just listened.

"Those weapons. As far as I can tell they're all quality control failures. You're selling weapons that won't even work properly. Tell me I'm wrong."

"You're right," Mary admitted with a shrug of the shoulders.

Alexei shook his head. "A proper little angel of death, you are."

"What do you want?" Mary asked - bored by his pointless chatter.

Alexei stood up and walked towards the door - turning as he said, "You'll know soon enough - my little Angel. You'll know soon enough."

The reference to Mary's personal call sign - ANGEL - sent shivers down her spine. He clearly knew way more than she had hoped.

And it was only a few weeks later that she discovered

what he wanted.

Mary had been watching the sunset on the horizon from the magnificent viewpoint of Victoria Peak - the lights of the buildings on the island and across the water in Kowloon and the New Territories, creating a glorious display that many Hong Kong residents and visitors alike have enjoyed over the years.

However, the peace and tranquillity was disturbed when her mobile phone buzzed with an encrypted message.

Mary stood in a quiet corner on the viewing deck - her hands uncharacteristically trembling, as she read and re-read the decrypted the message.

It was both a shocking and brutal message. It left nothing to the imagination.

Having been delivered as an encrypted file within a digital picture, separated from the encryption key that only she was privy to, it was as secure as any message could be.

Mary reluctantly concluded that the instructions were flawless. Even her personal call-sign, ANGEL, was correctly referenced at the beginning of each line.

Such was the seriousness of the content, she knew it would be headline news. This wasn't something you could do in the hope that it would go unnoticed.

And when it was done. When she had accomplished the unthinkable and it was all over, the whole world would pour scorn on the perpetrator - namely, her!

"Damn him," Mary muttered aloud, as she deleted the decoded message on her mobile phone. "This really will have to be planned meticulously."

Just thinking about it, horrified her. She knew there would be no second chance.

As soon as it became public - which would be almost immediately - there would be news stories followed by investigations, more investigations and then, even more investigations.

Investigations that would, inevitably, be conducted by some of the greatest minds on the planet.

She was also well aware that this could easily mark the end of her career - potentially her liberty - possibly even her life.

"Especially if everything else comes to light," she pondered. "And with the intense scrutiny that will undoubtedly follow, that's entirely possible. Especially if he's been leaking information."

Her thoughts paused for a moment.

Mary knew that she had no choice. She just didn't like it.

Alexei had been very clear. This was about power.

It was about proving control over her. Proving that she was a slave to someone his whim, where the penalty for failure was too horrible to contemplate.

And the penalty for success, wasn't that much better.

An uncharacteristic tear appeared in her left eye as she whispered rhetorically, "How in the world did I allow it to get this bad?"

Looking back at her mobile phone, Mary flicked through the Contacts, briefly stopping at Price - seeing the image of his face, whilst wondering whether to call and ask for his help.

"I can't," she thought. "This is too bad, even for him."

With the mobile phone safely stowed in her pocket, she just stared at the world in silence. Then, after a moment of reflection, she brushed her eye with the back of her hand, whilst thinking, "Maybe. Just maybe, there might be a way."

2. Innocent Victim?

Six months later....

Vitaly Isaev was a giant imposing figure. A veritable tower of a man. His formidable exterior lessened only marginally by a receding grey hairline and mature facial features.

On this occasion - an average English day that was scarcely indistinguishable from any other - Vitaly's broad shoulders were hunched forward in one of the many luxury stores of London's Bond Street.

He was leaning over a glass display cabinet, using a jeweller's loupe to magnify the fine details and engravings on a gold necklace - a gift for his wife as a celebration of their twenty-fifth wedding anniversary.

Some twenty feet behind him, outside the beautifully carpeted sales floor, the dark wood frame around the shop windows and panelled door gave the building a sturdy Georgian-like appearance. In many ways, it almost resembled the frontage of a grand family home of years gone by.

In reality, however, it was the home of an exclusive jeweller. A shop that only opened its doors to a very select group of people - Vitaly amongst them.

As Vitaly read the engraving - something that he had requested especially for his wife - the warm, peaceful atmosphere was brought to a sudden and abrupt end.

The shop front may have appeared to be sturdy, but it

was no match for the Toyota Landcruiser.

The 4X4 had been reinforced with large steel rams, enabling it to crash through the front wall and the window displays at speed.

Bricks and mortar were smashed to pieces, sending shards of masonry, wood and glass in all directions.

The vehicle came to a halt in the middle of the sales floor, knocking over a life-size bronze statue of the shop's original proprietor. A prized possession that was steeped in history - all a part of the glamour and appeal that provided an almost theatrical experience which continued to attract the rich and famous, as it had for over a hundred years.

The history and affection for the store, beloved by so many, meant nothing to the three hooded men who emerged from the vehicle.

Swinging large iron hammers, they smashed what remained of the glass displays, grabbing handfuls of the priceless jewellery whilst a fourth man just walked slowly around the room. A room that, in an instant, had been transformed from an awe-inspiring exhibition to something more resembling a building site.

Brandishing a large black baseball bat that he swung around menacingly, the fourth man was apparently undecided whether to strike anyone, or just terrify the shocked and disorientated staff and customers.

In the end, just as they left, Slavic Stepka used the baseball to land a single violent blow to only one person - Vitaly Isaev - who didn't even get to see his attacker. He'd been nursing an injury where a shard of glass had been embedded in to his right leg.

As the police and security services later observed when reviewing CCTV footage of the incident - that had been the blow containing the nerve agent.

At first glance, it looked like a smash-and-grab attack by a professional criminal gang. However, the pictures and subsequent autopsy of Vitaly's body told a very different story indeed.

The attack was premeditated murder and nothing less.

The baseball bat had a small blade fixed to one side. It was barely visible, but had clearly been used to deliver the poison.

And such was the potency of the nerve agent, it took only two minutes for Vitaly's eyes to turn white, as his entire body began to convulse.

The coroner later confirmed that, whilst his facial expression at death indicated excruciating pain, at around the same time he had also lost control of his voluntary bodily functions - shortly thereafter, the involuntary ones as well - his heart and breathing stopping just a few seconds later.

Death had been relatively quick. But as the coroner noted in his report, "It was a particularly cruel and unpleasant way for someone to die. The final moments of consciousness would have been truly horrific. Too horrible for us to even begin to contemplate."

The UK's Defence Science and Technology Laboratory, better known simply as Porton Down, later confirmed that his death had been caused by a VX-based nerve agent - a variation of one of the mostly deadly chemical weapons in existence.

Outlawed by the United Nations and, in theory at least, not stored in any country for anything other than defence and identification purposes by the likes of Porton Down, the agent is created by an extremely delicate and complex manufacturing process - in part just to create the chemical, and in part to prevent contamination - given that a pinhead of the liquid is sufficient to kill thousands of people.

As a result, the Porton Down scientists knew that it could have originated from one of only a handful of sources.

In this case, an exhaustive forensic and chemical analysis enabled them to narrow it down to a specific country.

Russia!

3. The Courier

The nerve agent attack sent the British security services in to a state of frenzy - closely followed by the British and international news media, who portrayed Vitaly Isaev's final moments in horrific, graphic detail on the front of newspapers and in hastily scheduled TV reports.

What the media didn't know, however, was that Vitaly, the now famous Russian London resident, had actually been working for the UK as a spy.

An ex-army Major and a product of the Soviet era, he had been assigned to finish his distinguished career peacefully at the Russian consulate in London.

At least, that was the official story. In reality, he was spying on behalf of Her Majesty's government, or to be more specific, SIS, aka MI6.

And that was another problem - although, not one that was discussed in public of course.

Nobody in SIS knew how he had been compromised. It had been one the most secretive relationships that they maintained.

All the intelligence Vitaly provided was routinely anonymised and attributed to other sources. The original data being subject to the strictest controls, consistently being labelled as TOP SECRET UK EYES ALPHA - thereby ensuring that only a handful of individuals were aware of the true source.

Even the SIS Chief was heard to comment, "What gave him away? We need to get better at handling these kinds of sources. These are the people who separate us from all the other intelligence services in the world."

In the short term, however, none of that mattered.

The immediate concern, and the topic that occupied everyone's mind, was the nerve agent. A weapon of mass destruction that had been used to murder a UK resident on the streets of the capital - London.

As a result, all non-critical surveillance was cancelled and those working on assignments abroad were told to return home unless there were exceptional or life-threatening reasons not to do so.

Even Price, whose role in SIS pretty much always meant operating outside the UK, was co-opted to a task force - the sole aim of which was to determine if any more of the nerve agent had been brought in to the UK. And if so, by whom and where.

Such was the seriousness, the Foreign Secretary who is, traditionally, the political leader and ultimate head of SIS, gave a briefing directly to the task force.

He said, "I want to know the individuals who brought it in. I want to know how they brought it in. I want to know if there is any more out there. And, you can't repeat this - but if the right situation presents itself, I want those individuals removed. Permanently."

Consequently, on a late damp evening just over three months after the initial attack, Price found himself standing in the shadows at the side of a nondescript road - a few yards away from a bus stop in one of London's many suburbs.

His plan had been to meet the courier - the man who, according to intelligence reports, was instrumental in the importation and transportation of the nerve agent.

Price was to pose as the courier's London contact with details of the next target. However, the courier had managed to lose his tail, leaving Price wondering if his own identity had been compromised as well.

If so, he could be in considerable danger. But, as he reflected, "Yeah. Whatever. That's just another of the less predictable parts of this job. One of a million others, all of which are designed to end my life before I can receive my pension."

Then, after a short pause, his thoughts continued with, "No more income tax though. I guess that's a positive."

Smiling inwardly at his own joke, Price just shrugged his shoulders and focused on the task.

In the end though, having sat in a bar in what appeared to be a futile attempt to complete the meeting, Price had finally given up and was heading home.

Despite being at a bus stop, he was actually waiting for a taxi. It just made a convenient place for the driver to stop.

It was a landmark and a place for the taxi to briefly park, in an otherwise gloomy road. Made even more so by the fact that, such was the late hour, all the shops and bars nearby had not only closed, they had switched their lights off as well.

That said, "Old habits die hard," Price mused as he noted that, without even thinking, he had walked to the best strategic position at the side of the road.

He was standing in an unlit corner with a clear view of his surroundings, whilst himself being very difficult to observe.

Another patron who was making her slightly drunken way home - a middle-aged lady he estimated - crossed the road ahead of him.

Her head was bowed, staring at a mobile phone that lit up in her hands.

She was evidently messaging someone whilst, for his part, Price just stood still - his hands in his pockets and his shoulders slightly hunched - a reaction to the cool damp breeze of the night.

It was then, despite being slightly weary from all the alcohol he had consumed, Price's senses made something switch inside his brain. His mind suddenly became alert as he heard an engine rev up.

Ordinarily, an engine revving wouldn't be a cause for concern. But something in his subconscious - perhaps as a result of all his years of training and hard-fought experience - made alarms bells ring in his head.

Price turned towards the noise, only to see a small motorbike. He guessed it was 125cc judging by the sound and its size.

Astride the bike were two hooded riders who swerved towards the lady and stopped with a loud screech.

One rider withdrew a machete and started slashing at the lady's arm, whilst the other grabbed the handbag which had been slung over her shoulder - swiping the mobile phone out of her hand at the same time.

Price hesitated for a second, cursing inwardly as he breathed in the cold air - again feeling the effects of the alcohol he'd consumed in the bar, dull his senses.

"What could I do? I didn't have a choice" he thought. "Sitting in the bar just drinking lemonade or a coffee would have drawn even more attention. It was bad enough sitting there on my own anyway."

As the attackers got back on their bike and its engine responded, Price snapped his thoughts back to the present - seeing the lady sprawled on the ground with blood gushing from her arm, where the blade had cut through her clothes and into her skin and bone.

Ordinarily, he would have rushed to her aid. But his emotions, probably another result of all the alcohol he'd been drinking, got the better of him.

Just as the bike moved away, Price withdrew his Smith and Wesson SW990L pistol, accessed by a false pocket in the left leg of his chinos.

Then he fired.

The noise of the unsuppressed bullet was almost like a car back-firing. It drowned out the bike's engine as well as the dull note of a night bus that was arriving on the far side of the road, some twenty yards away.

To an observer, it would have appeared to be an almost casual action, as Price didn't bother to take aim in the traditional sense. He just pointed and fired, apparently with little concern for accuracy.

It was an instinctive shot, destined for success as a result of the hundreds of hours of practise. And whilst Price may have appeared casual, the effect his gunshot had, was anything but.

The bullet struck the back of the bike's passenger dead-centre.

In a fraction of a second it ripped through skin and muscles, splintering his spine, causing immediate paralysis, followed by an explosion of blood that filled his lungs.

However, the devastation didn't stop there - the bullet still had plenty of energy. Its journey had only just begun.

Such was its momentum, it exited via the passenger's ribs, before entering the back of the driver.

Slightly left of centre at this point, it punctured the driver's heart, severing an artery, causing massive internal bleeding before finally coming to a halt just short of the forth rib.

The faster a bike is travelling, the more stable it is - it's the way the forces act on the vehicle.

However, despite knowing this, the fact that the first bullet hadn't brought the bike to an immediate halt caused Price to fire again a couple of seconds later.

Equally relaxed and instinctively well-aimed, the second bullet struck the back wheel - exploding it and sending the two men careering across the road, in to the path of the oncoming bus.

The bus finished the job for Price - not that the first bullet hadn't already been fatal to both men.

The bus driver stamped on his brake pedal, causing the front tyres to briefly skip on the slightly greasy road - the result of rain earlier in the day.

But it didn't help. The bikers' bodies were pinned to the tarmac and compressed as easily as swatting a fly.

Price remained perfectly calm, as he reached down and replaced the gun in its holster.

He knew that the screaming was inevitable, as a crowd of late-night pedestrians and passengers emerging from the bus, saw the bloodied remains of the men - crushed under the front wheels.

There was nothing he could do about that. And in any case, he felt no sympathy for thugs like them.

"If you're going to play a grown-up game, you can expect to receive a grown-up response," Price muttered to himself, before walking away - briefly stepping out of the shadows and turning a corner to a side street, whilst using his phone to cancel the taxi he'd been waiting for.

Then, as is the art of an experienced intelligence officer, he simply vanished from the scene - feeling significantly more awake than he had a few moments earlier.

Price knew it wouldn't be that easy though.

It was just a matter of time before the police found the bullets, matched them to their records and discovered they belonged to an SIS weapon. Indeed, he could already hear the sirens in the distance.

Very soon, ambulances would remove the bodies, the road would be closed and the evidence - namely his bullets - would be analysed by the police forensic department.

Sure, he was allowed to carry the gun. But it had been made very clear during the task force briefing a week earlier - only armed police units were allowed to use their weapons, unless the situation was absolutely unavoidable and essential to save lives.

In his head, he could already hear the SIS Chief saying, "What the hell were you thinking? That doesn't include low class scum like muggers Price! That's why we have the police and the courts and the judges!"

With that in mind, he phoned the SIS Chief of Staff, eliciting an immediate reply despite the late hour.

"What's up?"

"I've just seen someone shot."

"Go to bed. That's a police matter."

"Not entirely."

The Chief of Staff recognised Price's tone, and said, "I'm at home. Where are you?"

"About thirty minutes away?"

"I'll put the coffee on, you sound pissed."

Again, Price cursed to himself. He enjoyed drinking. He just hated how it impacted his actions sometimes. And on this occasion, it meant that all he could think of as a reply was, "Yeah. Not for long I can assure you."

Then he dropped the call as he hailed a passing black cab - one of London's famous taxis, who are legendary for their knowledge.

A little while later - a strong coffee in his hand, already half consumed - Price finally finished describing the evening's events - having recounted every detail as accurately as he could.

The Chief of Staff was clearly irritated by Price's story as he held out his hand and said, "Give me the gun."

Price handed it over without hesitation as the Chief of Staff said, "You lost this two weeks ago on a training exercise. The records will show that. You can collect a replacement from the armourer tomorrow."

Price nodded his gratitude. However, he knew that wouldn't be enough to make the problem go away. Sure, he was glad two nasty thieves were dead. But murder is murder and he needed an alibi - just in case someone found it suspicious.

So, he said, "Where was I tonight? We may need to answer that question."

The Chief of Staff nodded in disagreement, "It's most unlikely. These things are almost never questioned. As soon as the bullet is matched to you, they'll refer it to Special Branch - and they'll handle it with a phone call to the Chief."

Then, after a short pause he added, "But, given the task force and heightened security right now, I suppose there is a remote possibility. You're right, we need to be prepared for that."

Price didn't speak. He knew the Chief of Staff would give him an instruction. So, he just waited - eventually, a little surprised by what he heard.

"Go now. Find a prostitute and pay her well. That's your

alibi."

Price laughed as the Chief of Staff smiled back, before adding, considerably more assertively, "Go!"

Price didn't reply - he just put his coffee mug down and left. Whilst for his part, the Chief of Staff picked up his direct line to the SIS headquarters at Vauxhall Cross - his encrypted link that ensured there could be no eavesdroppers as he spoke to the duty manager.

"I need a favour. Price lost his weapon two weeks ago during a training exercise. He forgot to mention it earlier and I need the records updated to reflect that."

The duty manager smiled as he logged in to the SIS records system and retrieved the records relating to Price's Smith and Wesson - immediately changing the entry to record it as having been lost two weeks earlier whilst participating in a confidential training exercise in the Welsh mountains - somewhere far too vast to search with any likelihood of success.

Then he said, "You're mistaken. The records already do show that Sir."

Now the Chief of Staff smiled as he said, "Thank you. Goodnight."

"Night Sir."

A few miles away in London's Soho district, the conversation was taking a very different turn.

"I'm Elliot, how are you?"

"Take me home and I'll show you honey."

Price smiled, "On one condition."

"What?"

"I need you to send a message to one of your friends telling them that you've been with me all evening."

"Why?"

"I know it sounds strange, but could you tell someone that we met at eight this evening and you've been with me ever since. Tell someone, frankly anyone, please, because I just need it on record."

"You're crazy!"

Price sighed, "I'll pay you well. Just send a message to that effect please. Tell someone you've been having a really great time. It's important. Please?"

"But it's not true."

Price laughed, "Let's not confuse ourselves and worry about such luxuries as the truth. After all, you won't be telling the truth in half an hour when you tell me I'm wonderful in bed."

"You might be. How do I know?"

Price smiled, "I can assure you I'm not. And I snore. In any case, it doesn't matter. Just send the damn message and I'll give you some cash!"

When she didn't reply, Price realised he had probably been too aggressive. So, he tried again, adopting a softer tone to see if that worked.

"Please send the message for me. I'd really appreciate it."

The girl looked at Price as if he was mad, which he knew was to be expected. Then, much to his relief, she sent a message and showed it to him.

Price would have preferred not to have been described as a fucking arsehole. But, thinking back to the incident later the same evening, he concluded that, "Needs must. And anyway, it's probably not entirely inaccurate. Credit where it's due. She's clearly a good judge of character."

Needless to say, he hailed a taxi and a short while later was receiving the benefit of her experience.

For his part, Price just watched her head move up and down on his lap, thinking, "Damn, I had meant to buy some milk from a 7-11 on the way home. I must sort that out tomorrow, otherwise I'll have to drink my coffee black - and that's never a good thing."

The girl must have realised that Price wasn't paying attention, because a few seconds later she stopped what she was doing and looked up at him.

Making eye contact, Price smiled as he said, "You can't say I didn't warn you."

Whilst Price ended his evening amused by his own joke, having already forgotten about the bikers - thousands of miles away in darkest Russia the imposing figure of Slavic Stepka, cursed.

Unaware that his brother had been killed (by Price) whilst attempting to rob someone - all he knew was, he'd lost contact with his brother, who had been working on a covert operation in Britain.

Given the dangers of the operation, and the fact that he had been the one who had recommended his brother for the task, they had spoken every day.

Then suddenly, nothing. The phone didn't even ring.

Even more disturbingly, his commanding officer in Russia's FSB - the Federal Security Service - had instructed him to eliminate an enemy of the state.

That in itself wasn't unusual. As an experienced FSB operative, he had undertaken numerous covert operations.

The disturbing part was - the person he had to kill was the very same person he had been spying for illegally - as a double-agent.

However, he knew he had no choice. It was a case of, kill Mary or be killed. Or even worse.

With that in mind, he demanded a meeting.

4. Let This Be A Lesson

Standing in the shadow of a doorway, desperately trying not to shiver in the icy winter, Mary had one hand in her pocket clasping her gun - whilst the other held on to a night vision monocular.

The monocular was her preferred choice over the more traditional binoculars, as it allowed one of her eyes to remain adjusted to the darkness whilst the other viewed the bright infrared-lit scene in the eyepiece.

Mary knew it was an extremely risky meeting. She had entered Russia illegally, having been forced to leave China's Moscow consulate many years earlier, as a suspected spy.

At the time, there had been repeated protests from the Chinese government and, as is always the case in these situations, a number retaliatory actions that had inevitably led to Russian overseas embassy staff being required to leave China.

However, behind closed doors, everyone knew that Russia got it right. She was a spy and had been the mastermind behind the death of a Russian FSB agent.

As Mary later described it, "The FSB killed a Chinese consulate official. Sure, everyone knows it was a case of mistaken identity. But that does not excuse their action, and it should not go unpunished."

And it hadn't.

Mary had been brutally efficient in tracking down the executioner and executing him - albeit, rather cruelly, as she reluctantly admitted sometime later when questioned by her superiors.

"It's only what they would have done if the situation was reversed," she replied. Adding, "It isn't the first time a body has been repatriated in lots of pieces the size of a shoe box. Although, I do admit, starting with his genitals was perhaps a little unconventional."

That said, irrespective of who was right or wrong, the incident left Mary barred from Russia for life.

Whilst Russia had obeyed international law and she had been afforded her diplomatic rights - thereby being deported with the immunity it provided - the Russian Ambassador in Beijing had made it very clear. If she entered Russia again, the authorities would not be quite so forgiving. She would be held accountable for murder.

And he left nothing to their imagination. They would not waste time with formalities such as a trial. She would be sentenced behind closed doors with the harshest possible result.

On this occasion though, Mary had very little choice.

Having been originally recruited by what you might describe as the traditional route - a euphemism for blackmail - Slavic Stepka, an agent she'd been handling for several years, had suddenly decided to become brave. He had even given Mary an ultimatum. They were to meet in Russia or it was over.

"You can do whatever you want," he had said, with no apparent concern for the consequences if she chose to reveal that he was a double-agent.

When challenged about why he was so insistent the meeting had to be in Russia, he had cited problems with his travel documents - something Mary didn't believe for even a second.

But she also knew, as did he, that she had no choice.

He had been one of a number of agents that, over the years, had led to Mary's meteoric rise within the Chinese security service. So, she didn't want to just walk away - indeed, she couldn't afford to. It was her professional reputation that was at stake.

With that in mind and with all considerations suitably assessed, reviewed, planned and planned again, she judged that one meeting was worth the risk and chose her meeting place very carefully.

It was to be the location of the newly constructed border crossing between China and Russia - the Nizhneleninskoye-Tongjiang bridge which crosses the Amur River - a natural boundary separating the two countries in the far northeast corner of Russia and China.

Due to open later in the year, the construction work meant there were frequent, and often quite poorly-tracked, border crossings by workers.

In other words, it was a perfect cover.

From Russia's perspective, Mary would be just another one of the dozens of project managers that were there to supervise the work.

After some hastily arranged phone calls, her site pass was prepared and the site manager on the China side of the bridge was informed that Mary would be observing their activities and providing governmental oversight.

In other words, she was to be left alone and not to be questioned in any way - ever!

That said, the weather was not on her side.

The temperature had taken a sudden turn for the worst the previous week and that, combined with the onset of snow, meant that the river was completely frozen over. So much so that, work on the bridge had slowed to a snail's pace.

Nizhneleninskoye is a small rural community that sits a couple of miles away from its larger brother - the district administrative centre, Leninskoye, where Mary had rented a room a few days earlier in order to familiarise herself with the surroundings.

That essential preparation ultimately led her to select the precise meeting place - an unoccupied and somewhat dilapidated corrugated-iron barn, some twenty yards north of a major road junction.

It not only provided her with some protection from the elements - particularly the freezing wind that stung as it struck her face - but it also gave her a clear view of anyone else approaching her position.

Most importantly, it was also not far from the river, which flowed east-west a couple-of-hundred yards to her south - just one of her potential escape routes if things didn't go as planned.

As Mary nervously scanned her surroundings with her monocular, a few wild cats and stray dogs showed up as well as some people in a building a few hundred yards away. Otherwise, the infrared scene in the viewfinder was a sea of light blue - an all too clear indication of the sub-zero temperatures.

The lack of activity was to be expected. It was very late at night and Mary was an hour early for the meeting.

Experience had taught her that it was best to be early.

The last thing she needed was a surprise.

Mary had prepared multiple contingency plans and began to replay them all in her mind as she continued to survey her surroundings - only disturbed by the occasional passing car and a group of people - around ten or twelve she estimated - who had gathered near the waterfront directly to her south.

She presumed they had been working on the bridge and only really caught her attention because they were huddled around a burning barrel. They were warming their hands - apparently laughing about something.

Mary glanced at her watch.

There were still forty-five minutes to go and nobody else in sight.

She reassured herself that was OK. Her contact would probably be precise, if his past track record was anything to go by.

As the wind sent chills through her body, Mary just waited patiently - occasionally exercising her legs to keep the joints warm, whilst constantly scanning for movement and listening to every sound, even the creaking of the barn's internal wooden frame as the wind lashed at its flat sides.

This was always the most dangerous part of a meeting. The uncertainty, right up until code words are exchanged and an understanding and mutual trust has been reached.

"Even then," she reflected, "You can never completely relax. It's not over until you are home and walking in your front door."

Mary checked her gun. It was loaded and ready to fire. Then she checked it again - just to be sure - her sense of trepidation growing with every minute.

Mary didn't know why she felt so nervous. This wasn't an unfamiliar assignment. She'd managed countless agents over the years - often, in considerably more hazardous circumstances.

Another glance at her watch.

Thirty minutes to go now and the workers seemed to be packing up. Certainly, they were extinguishing the fire.

"Why do that so soon after arriving," she wondered.

Mary wasn't sure why, but something didn't seem right about that. It was quite late and whilst the fire had been reasonably intense, in the present weather conditions it would have easily burned itself out.

"Why go to all the trouble of extinguishing it," she thought. "After all, it's on concrete, nowhere near anything else and with snow forecast. Why bother? Unless of course, they know I'm watching and want to keep my attention."

With that in mind, Mary scanned all directions with her monocular again, still looking for infrared patterns to indicate her agent was arriving.

There was nothing. Just a sea of black and cold blue.

"Stop it," she told herself. "Your mind is playing tricks on you and that's detrimental to performance," as she noticed that the workers appeared to have dispersed and had walked away from the waterfront.

She presumed they were heading home - back to their temporary accommodation blocks, which had been constructed on the outskirts of the town - some to the west and some to the east.

Another glance at her watch.

Fifteen minutes to go now.

"What's that," Mary thought as she switched back to the monocular - noticing that the workers were not walking to their accommodation blocks at all. They had spread out and appeared to be heading in her direction.

Mary's heart started to beat faster as she scanned the road in front and behind the barn to the north.

Suddenly, there were lots of bright dots - all of which were getting steadily brighter and heading towards her position.

"Damnit! It was a trap after all. They must have been hiding in the snow to avoid detection," she mused as she checked back on the workers, who had now started to run - albeit quite slowly.

She was cut off from the river to her south - her first choice of escape - and was now surrounded on the other three sides.

She could only presume that, like her, they had used night

vision to detect her presence and had, as she had wondered, attempted to use the workers as a distraction. At least, she hoped so.

Letting go of the gun, that she had been thinking of using to execute her agent if the meeting didn't go as planned, Mary removed a remote control from her jacket pocket.

"Timing is everything," she thought, as she continued watching what she estimated were around thirty targets approaching from all directions.

"Too soon and they'll scatter. Too late and it's all a waste."

At first, not surprisingly, her contacts - or as she now viewed them, targets - were quite spread out. But as they moved in on her position they, necessarily, had to close-in on each other. Indeed, they were getting quite close now, in every sense - converging from all directions.

Mary's heart was beating extremely fast. It was screaming at her brain to order her legs to run and run hard. But she stayed still, despite noting that they were all armed - the AK47's in their hands were quite unmistakable.

"Just a few more seconds. Just a few more seconds," she told herself.

Her heart was throbbing now. She could feel the blood pulsing through her body. This was it. One mistake and it was all for nothing. She would be just another dead spy.

"Control it," she told herself. "Control it. It's just a task. Just a task," she repeated in her head. "Although, that's quite a lot easier said than done," she reminded herself - almost making herself laugh as a means to reduce the stress.

As the targets came in to view - this time without the benefit of the infrared monocular that she had clipped back on to her belt - Mary pushed the button on the remote control.

The charges she had placed along the south side of the road between her and the waterfront, and, to the north behind the barn that now provided protection for her back, erupted.

To the south, the men that had posed as workers burst in to flames.

Mary had chosen incendiary-type explosives as opposed to the more traditional shrapnel-based option.

Firstly, because she needed to make it impossible to use infrared night vision and, therefore, more difficult to follow her escape - which bright flames would do - and secondly because, she hoped the horror of watching people burning alive would act as a distraction.

"Slightly evil and most definitely a painful way to go," Mary noted. Then, with a total lack of concern, she also noted that the devices had worked well.

As she watched the men fall to the ground, engulfed in flames and screaming in agony as their skin blistered and burned, Mary even managed to muster a smile whilst thinking, "Let this be a lesson."

To her north, the explosions behind the barn were far more traditional - with shrapnel tearing through skin and bones, ironically setting fire to the internal wooden frame of the barn in the process - thereby creating an even larger infrared scene which Mary hadn't specifically intended, but was most grateful for nevertheless.

Mary dropped the remote control and reached in to her pocket for a second device. Then, lowering the hood from her coat so that she had a clearer - albeit colder - view of her surroundings, she took off like a scolded cat.

Mary ran straight across the road, past the burning bodies, and in to a field where the frozen grass gave her winter boots traction - enabling her to sprint as fast as her legs would take her.

Turning to the west, running parallel to the river, Mary could hear shouting and screaming behind her.

Shouting from people presumably pointing towards her, and screaming as local residents emerged to see people burning alive in their streets.

"Welcome to Russia," she said to herself - smiling as she heard the sound of car engines starting up and revving.

Mary had assumed they wouldn't run after her. It would be a truly brutal sprint.

She was legendary in her service for her unbelievable fitness and astonishing speed. But this was destined to be nothing less than devastating. Even as Mary had planned her escape, she had questioned herself, "Would this route even be survivable in the current conditions?"

She had three miles to cover - on foot - at night - in sub-zero temperatures that would attack her lungs like knives, as she sucked in the cold air as fast as she could.

Mary's only consolation was that the snow and a full moon provided a small amount of natural light that allowed her to clearly see some deep ditches, which she easily jumped across - fully in the knowledge that, if they did choose to follow her across the fields by car, they would definitely get stuck.

But she knew they wouldn't do that.

She knew exactly where they would converge, and that would be at Leninskoye.

There are two road routes from Nizhneleninskoye to Leninskoye. One follows the river to the south, which is the shortest most direct route, and a far longer circuitous route to the north.

Mary knew that they would see her running west and take the road by the river.

And sure enough, as she looked to her left, she could see the cars speed past her just as she pressed the button on her second remote control.

The resulting explosion was so great that, at the point of impact, it removed any evidence the road had even existed - destroying all the vehicles and leaving a large crater where they had once been.

However, whilst she would have loved to have stopped and admired the effects of her work, Mary ran on - eventually reaching the southerly outskirts of Leninskoye.

As she stood, almost bent double from pain, coughing violently and trying to catch her breath by the edge of the frozen river, Mary knew that she was about to make the most dangerous part of her escape.

She would be crossing the river, where she would have no cover whatsoever.

If, by some bad luck, they had managed to get there before her, or happened to have armed security guards ready and waiting, she didn't stand a chance.

She also knew that it was a risk she had to take. A risk that she had weighed up and planned for. A risk that was a part of the job.

So, relegating the thoughts to the back of her mind, Mary retrieved the snowmobile she had rented a week earlier and quickly scanned the horizon one last time with her monocular.

Sure enough, they were there - but didn't seem to be very close - at least, not close enough to be a concern.

There appeared to be two main groups. The survivors from the first explosions by the barn who, on seeing the cars destroyed, had set off on foot - and a bunch of other vehicles - survivors from the second explosion, who had turned back and were now taking the longer route to the north.

Either way, she estimated they were about five to ten minutes behind her.

"Just about enough," she decided, as she kicked the snowmobile in to life and checked everything was working before heading out across the river.

It was extremely rough going. Certainly not a smooth ice rink as she would have liked.

Such was the brutality of the weather, it had frozen the water in to a series of peaks and troughs, including some particularly sharp spikes that she had to avoid for fear of damaging the snowmobile's tracks.

All things considered, it meant she had to proceed exceedingly carefully and slowly - especially with only the moonlight for guidance, because there was no way she could risk using the snowmobile's lights.

"I only have to get to the far side and I'm home," Mary reminded herself.

But it was destined to be close. At least one of the survivors had managed to catch up - quite a lot faster than she had anticipated.

Just as she approached the far side of the river, seeing the welcoming arms of her colleagues in the distance, Mary heard a familiar Russian voice call out.

It was Slavic Stepka - the very person she had been there to meet.

Mary grabbed at the brake and leapt behind the snowmobile, crouching down to take cover - fully expecting to hear shots ring out any second.

She knew only too well that, for a well-trained sniper with night-vision, she was a victim in the making. The snowmobile provided visible cover. But, if they had infrared or ultraviolet scanners and a sniper's rifle, she didn't stand a chance. It would be game over.

To her surprise though, no bullets were fired.

"Perhaps they're not quite as organised as I thought," she wondered, as she withdrew her gun and shouted back, "Mu-dak," - a Russian translation of the insult, "Dickhead."

It elicited an almost immediate reply that she didn't bother to comprehend, as that wasn't why she had shouted.

Instead, Mary just closed her eyes and focused on the sound and direction of the angry response - in the process determining a fairly precise position for the voice.

Then, with that memory printed on her mind - her eyes still closed - she raised her gun and fired. Then again and again and again.

An accomplished marksman, Mary was sure that she heard a cry of pain. Although, when the adrenalin is pumping and you're hearing the bullets expelled from the weapon inches from your head, it's difficult to tell.

But as she finished the entire magazine, without receiving even a single shot in return, Mary crawled away and back in to the safety of her home country - very relieved to have survived the night.

5. Never Again

Slavic Stepka clutched his leg where one of Mary's shots had managed to reach its target - albeit a shot that, fortunately for him, had missed all his vital organs.

He would have liked to return fire. But, by the time he had managed to compose himself, after being struck by the somewhat unexpected bullet, he could see that Mary was well beyond the range of his gun. At least, she was if he was hoping for any degree of accuracy.

He didn't really care that much. Crouched down in the frozen ice and snow at the bank of the river, that was now the least of his worries.

A part of him almost wished Mary's shot had been fatal.

"At least that way, it would have brought this nightmare to an end," he decided.

His problem was that he'd failed to kill her. And as a direct result of that, he now faced the very real prospect of being returned to Black Dolphin.

Before he could move, he felt the unmistakable push of a gun barrel in the centre of his spine. A feeling that filled his mind with horror.

A commanding voice bellowed in to his ears, "Prisoner 57263 get to your feet this instant."

Still clutching the bullet wound, he stood up.

It wasn't wise to disobey these people, even if it did mean

suffering the agonising pain in his leg. That was nothing compared to what they could inflict if they chose to.

His hands were immediately locked behind his back, as he was marched to a waiting prison vehicle.

Not that he could see the vehicle - a black shroud covered his eyes and he was forced in to a downward facing position so that his head was below the height of his shoulders - all standard operating procedure at Black Dolphin, to maintain control over a prisoner's movement and prevent them from seeing where they were, or indeed, the layout of the prison itself.

Feelings of dread washed through his body. His mind was racing - terrified, even traumatised, by the very real prospect of returning there.

He couldn't stop thinking, "I can't go back. I can't go back to Black Dolphin."

The drive seemed to take forever.

Minutes became hours - although, how many hours, he had no way of knowing.

Despite being locked in a stress position and bolted to a wooden bench, the fatigue of the night eventually took its toll and he fell asleep.

When he woke-up an unknown period of time later, his joints and muscles were agonisingly painful from the hours of constriction.

He didn't speak though.

He processed it all inside his head. These people didn't respond well to questions or complaints. So, he just suffered the pain internally and remained silent.

The sun was high in the sky by the time the truck eventually stopped and he heard the engine switch off. Not that he could see out. His only view was the bright white lines that shone through the small gaps around the doors.

Strangely, something told him that this wasn't a fuel stop. It felt and, judging by the guards moving around outside, sounded like they had actually arrived at their destination.

"Surely, I can't have slept that long," he thought. "We were too far away for this to be Black Dolphin already. There's no way. That would mean a flight."

He was right.

As Prisoner 57263, as he was now known, stepped down from the back of the vehicle, now chained to two armed guards, whilst being followed by a further four more, he saw his home town.

Right in front of him, he could see the imposing grey tower block where he lived in a modest two-bedroom apartment.

Breaking with the usual Black Dolphin procedures, he was marched fully upright across the road and to the front of his apartment block - grateful for the chance to breath the fresh air of the day and take in the surroundings.

The statue at the nearby intersection always made him smile, and this day was no exception. The snow had eroded part of the figure's abdomen, somehow creating a strange profile that, from some angles, was quite obscene

- and amusing at the same time.

Then there was his favourite coffee shop - brightly lit up in the distance. Not that he really cared about the coffee. His interest was more the Slovakian lady who habitually wore t-shirts two sizes too small.

Not that he ever complained. It had often been one of the highlights of his day.

"I'm back home," he thought, whilst hardly being able to believe it - wondering why he had been brought there.

Two more guards were waiting outside his apartment, as his wrists were set free for the first time since leaving the river bank - although, how long ago that was, he couldn't tell.

Something definitely did not feel right - to the point that, he began to wonder if he had been drugged. Certainly, he had been given a drink soon after they set off.

"Perhaps that wasn't just water," he speculated as his head started to throb - the pain being a sure sign that he had consumed something his body wasn't happy with.

An officer opened the front door and waived him inside, where they arrived at his small living room - a simple, sparsely decorated box room - the only large features being a brown leather sofa that faced a flat screen TV which was fixed to the opposite wall, next to a door that led off to the small kitchen, utility room and bedrooms.

The officer in charge spoke for the first time.

"Prisoner 57263, you are under house arrest, pending your transfer back to prison. Until further notice, you may not leave. If you attempt to leave you will be shot. Do you understand?"

A simple nod sufficed as a reply. It was clear they were not joking. So, once the guards had left and his front door was closed, he sat down and switched on the TV.

Something was very wrong. He was beginning to feel lightheaded.

"What day is it?" he wondered - only to find, to his horror, that he had actually been travelling for several days.

Holding his head in his hands, in despair, he thought, "No way. How can that be?" as the realisation that he was unable to explain several days of his life, slow began to sink in to his brain.

"At least that explains the way I feel," he decided - not that it really provided any comfort.

It confirmed, however, that he had most definitely been drugged. And judging by the pain in his joints, had evidently been subject to some kind of interrogation as well.

Initially, he had assumed the muscle pains were the result of being fastened in a fixed position in the transport vehicle for an extended period of time. But as he relaxed, more and more bruises started to appear.

It felt like he had been repeatedly beaten.

Turning to the news channel, he wondered if Mary's escape and the carnage she had caused had attracted any attention. But after searching news articles for the past week, he wasn't in the least bit surprised to discover that it hadn't been considered newsworthy.

Even if the explosions had been reported, he fully expected them to be attributed to something else - most likely a gas leak, as that was the FSB's usual excuse in these situations.

Much to his surprise, the majority of the international news seemed to be a report about two bikers that had attacked an elderly lady, before being killed in an accident with a bus in London.

Undecided as to why it warranted so much reporting, he was about to change channel when the faces of the deceased were flashed on the screen.

The picture of the bike's driver made him freeze, as tears instantly filled his eyes.

Now he knew why his brother had not picked up his phone.

His mind started racing. This couldn't be a coincidence.

"A murder in London whilst I'm unconscious and then they threaten to send me back to Black Dolphin. What did I say whilst they had me drugged?" he wondered.

"Never," he thought. "I would never give him up! But with drugs, who knows what I did?"

Pausing for thought, he walked in to the kitchen and retrieved a bottle of vodka - pouring himself a shot and swallowing it in a single mouthful before filling the glass for a second time and walking back to the lounge - this time feeling a searing pain in his leg from the bullet wound.

Walking in to the bathroom, he dropped his trousers with the intention of treating the injury - only to find that it had already been treated. Indeed, it was covered in a fresh bandage. So, he returned to the lounge.

"How can this be? Who killed him?" he wondered as he sat on the sofa, contemplating his alternatives.

The news report said that the biker was killed after a hit-and-run theft went wrong.

Whilst he knew his brother was undisciplined and might do something like that, he also knew the real reason for his presence in London - that was far more serious.

After a few minutes of silence, he decided, "I must find out. I have to go. I have to escape. Tonight, under the cover of darkness. I can't go back to prison. And now they do this!"

As he emptied the second glass of vodka - once again in single mouthful - he thought, "They will pay. They will all pay for this! All of them! I will hunt them all down and they will all die! Especially her!"

Sure enough, less than six hours later the alarms were sounded. Although, they were not alarms in what you would consider the traditional sense.

These were emergency alert signals sent to all the security staff at Russia's borders and ports, as well as security stations across the country.

One senior official was heard to remark, "This search is completely pointless. He has gone. He won't surface until he wants to be found. We have trained him far too well. I told you we should have transferred him directly to prison. Delaying the inevitable just gave him an escape route."

And he was right.

Within a matter of hours, Slavic Stepka - aka Prisoner 57263 - was in a different country. He was travelling under a different name with a new, deadly mission all of his own.

6. An Embittered End

The brutality was the worst part.

The restaurant, a family run Italian, had been full at the time. Its usual mixture of business men, women and families - all enjoying the food and decor of the small dining room that was adorned with pictures and memoirs from the owner's home in the Italian Alps region of Valle d'Aosta.

It was a home-like atmosphere. The only sound, aside from the chatter of the guests, was their pianist, who casually played a string of classic songs in one corner of the room. The other corner, opposite the two either side of the entrance, was occupied by a large impressive kitchen that was open to the view of the guests, who delighted in the occasional flash of flames, when the chef added some liquor to flambé a dish - thereby enhancing the flavour whilst burning off some of the alcohol.

Anyone looking at the dining room, and the people within, would have been delighted by the pleasure it provided. They would have seen families celebrating special occasions, business people celebrating their successes, others discussing their plans for future success and dedicated food lovers admiring the skills of the chef - all smiling and laughing and enjoying both their company, as well as everything the restaurant provided for them.

As the head chef was often heard to say, as he walked amongst the guests in between orders, "Our pleasure is in serving the best food to you in a place that we hope you can almost think of as a second home."

Then it all changed.

The figure was dressed almost entirely in black - his face being covered by a grey scarf, leaving only the contrasting colour of his grey-blue eyes showing.

Even his dark hair, slightly tanned skin and unshaven look, matched his carefully chosen attire.

From the pictures on the CCTV cameras, the police later concluded that he was probably an ex-soldier.

Certainly, the way he moved around the room and the precision of his actions suggested that, despite his unkempt looks that were in stark contrast to the unmistakably expensive leather coat, he was most definitely a professional.

As he walked through the door, carefully avoiding the direct gaze of the CCTV cameras, the restaurant's maître d' approached him like any other guest - only to be aggressively pushed aside.

A group of business men seated in the corner near the pianist were the first victims, as the stranger's swiftly drawn sub-machine gun methodically worked its way around the room.

The suppressed thuds of the shots - the result of a large silencer fitting - were initially obscured by the shrieks and screams of the restaurant guests, which gradually subsided as the bullets took effect - tearing through clothing and skin, turning internal organs into shreds of their former selves, leaving a trail of blood in their wake.

Sadly, that was only the beginning of the nightmare.

On seeing the carnage, the brave chef ran out of the kitchen brandishing a large carving knife. But that only served to make the stranger switch to his other weapon - the one that, quite unbelievably, was even worse.

He drew a sword that had been concealed under his long coat. A large curved blade, that was in some ways reminiscent of a medieval scimitar.

The chef turned to run away, but the stranger was faster and stronger. His raised arm came crashing down - the blade cutting in to the chef's back - slicing through his skin and bone in a single swift movement before turning on the guests - most of whom were already either dead or dying.

He didn't seem to care though.

No man, woman or child was left untouched as he severed limbs with brutal efficiency - in the process, changing the beautifully carpeted floor in to a sea of blood.

Then, just as quickly as he had destroyed their lives, he was gone.

The police appealed for witnesses, in the hope that someone had seen the stranger enter or leave the restaurant - but there were very few responses.

In the end, the only real lead was a pedestrian who reported seeing a stranger driving away in a car. But after a lengthy search, the police only found a burning wreck of a vehicle that provided no usable evidence.

7. Steak A Dozen Ways

Several weeks had passed since Vitaly Isaev's murder.

There didn't appear to be a trace of any more nerve agent entering Britain, so the public focus was steadily shifting. Even the online and TV press appeared to have moved on to their next big news story.

Price, meanwhile, was taking advantage of the well-earned downtime to unwind between assignments - whilst at the same time practising one of his favourite pastimes.

Cooking steak.

He considered it to be an extremely fine line between an undercooked rare steak, which would be red and bloody in the middle - something he didn't particularly enjoy - and his favourite medium-rare steak, that was hot throughout, whilst also being red in the middle but not too bloody.

Just as he placed what he considered to be his best effort to-date on a plate, the phone rang.

Rather unusually, it was the SIS Chief himself.

"Hello Price."

Price recognised his voice in an instant.

"Sir, this is a surprise. How can I help?"

"We appear to have a rather unusual situation that calls for your unique skills. Operations room as quick as you can please."

"On my way Sir," was Price's reply as he hurriedly changed in to more appropriate clothing and then, as he was about to walk out the door, picked up two slices of bread and slid his perfectly cooked sirloin steak between them.

"This is just wrong," he thought as he took a large bite from what had just become a sirloin steak sandwich.

"That's life I guess. Needs must," he thought, as he drove in to central London to the famous SIS building at Vauxhall Cross.

Such was the traffic, or lack of it, Price took his last bite of the sandwich as he entered the SIS operations room, from where all major projects and activities are viewed and controlled - as a result, slightly slurring his greeting due to a mouthful of food. "Errvning."

The Chief nodded in recognition of Price's arrival. Then, the smallest glance to his left gave the Chief of Staff the cue to begin the briefing.

CCTV footage from the Italian restaurant played on the giant screen at one end of the room as the Chief of Staff provided some commentary.

"You'll have seen this in the news Price. Two days ago, in less than three minutes, a professional assassin wiped out an entire restaurant full of men, women and children."

Price just nodded, but didn't speak.

"At first glance, we thought it was possibly an ex-soldier who'd turned bad - perhaps due to post-traumatic stress. However, as we began to identify the victims, we realised there was rather more to it than that. Way more than you might think at first glance."

"Or rather," the Chief added - only to be interrupted again by the Chief of Staff.

"We identified someone who managed to escape. The only person in the room who did escape, by the way."

Price quickly swallowed the last piece of food as he studied the images. Then, just as the Chief of Staff was about to speak again, he said, "Stop! That business man in the corner. I know him."

This time the Chief spoke in a sombre tone. "Yes. It's Townsend, with some make-up to disguise him to a stranger. He was meeting an informant."

Price's look of disbelief was unmistakable, "Did he get out?"

"No Price. Nobody you can see in that picture of the room survived. I'm sorry," replied the Chief. "I know you two were good friends."

"Bastard!"

Price's uncharacteristic shout echoed around the room. Evidence of their close friendship - built on their history as former Paras, as those who served in the Royal Parachute Regiment refer to themselves.

The room fell silent, apart from the sound track that accompanied the CCTV footage, as they watched the scene unfold.

Even Price, who was used to seeing people die, grimaced as the killer moved at incredible speed around the room -

hacking the limbs off innocent dying or dead people, in the process.

He was horrified that even the children were brutalised.

Then, whilst the Chief and Chief of Staff stood silently, they noticed Price's expression change. He almost smiled.

"What is it?" the Chief asked.

"He's clearly sick and yet clearly a professional. I mean, look at the way he moves for a start - and the sheer strength of the man."

"But?" the Chief of Staff asked.

Price continued, "As one professional to another, I'd say he's sloppy. We all know rule number one on a job like that. There should be nothing to identify you. No identifying clothing, belongings or behaviour."

"So? What are you saying?"

Price's mind was suddenly bursting with energy - fully engaged, with his subconscious working furiously to figure out how to get back at the killer for the murder of his friend.

But he didn't let that delay his reply.

"Look at those earpieces. At first glance, you would think they're for communication, as they are military style fittings. But actually, that's just misdirection. If I'm not mistaken, he's listening to music. It's clearly audible in the background - and it must be bloody loud in his ears if the CCTV managed to pick it up."

"It could be from the restaurant," the Chief of Staff was quick to reply.

Price nodded, "No Sir. No way. Look. There's a pianist. You don't have a guy playing the piano and have the radio on. When he shot the pianist, he also killed the music. So, we must be hearing what he's hearing."

Without waiting for a reply, Price looked across to one of the operators who had been controlling the video.

"See if you can enhance that sound. Try and take out everything but the music if you can please."

A few seconds later, the music played out.

"I approve," Price remarked. "Jazz suite number two by Shostakovich. A favourite of mine as well."

Turning back to the operator he said, "Search every database on the planet and see if there's any known sick bastards that like it."

Then, after a brief pause, he added, "Aside from me that is, obviously."

"Why on earth?" the Chief of Staff started to ask.

"Because he's crazy," Price interrupted. "I agree it's a long shot. But, it also might just give him away if we're lucky."

The room fell silent again, then the Chief and Chief of Staff exchanged glances.

This time it was Price's turn to ask, "What do you two know that I don't?"

"As I indicated, one person did escape," the Chief of Staff replied. "So, as you'd expect we've enhanced the pictures. And well."

Price was stunned.

"That's Mary!"

"Yes. It does rather look like your girlfriend."

"What's a member of the Chinese intelligence service who is routinely stationed in Hong Kong doing in a London restaurant that's being attacked by a nutcase? That cannot be a coincidence!"

The Chief smiled as he said, "That was our thinking as well Price. We thought you might be able to throw some light on the matter."

"Well quite. I can see why you might say that Sir. And that explains why you called me here tonight, for what would normally be considered a police matter. I'd have done the same in your shoes. Frankly, I am a bit surprised she didn't at least say hello, since she was in the country."

"You need to see her escape," the Chief continued, as he nodded to the operator. "It's what you might call selfish."

Price frowned at the Chief before turning back to the video screen again.

It was extremely difficult to identify her initially. She was seated in a corner where the CCTV did not have a particularly good view and the lighting was poor.

"That was very well planned and entirely deliberate," Price thought.

"It's poor lighting in that part of the room," the Chief of Staff added - just as Price smiled, commenting, "She's not only good in bed Sir."

The video played again from the beginning - now with the contrast settings adjusted to highlight Mary's seat.

The instant the dark stranger entered the restaurant, Mary appeared to drop something on the floor and crawled under the table to retrieve it.

Then, as the bloody scene unfolded, she vanished. The only evidence of her escape being a brief glimpse of her leg as she slowly but surely crawled unobtrusively out of the restaurant via a back door, accessed via the kitchen.

Price frowned again, "Who was she with?"

The Chief of Staff glanced at his notes.

"Embassy staff mostly. Some of them known to us. Others were recent additions. Nothing particularly suspicious there. It was probably just dinner with a bunch of people who worked together."

"She didn't bother to warn any of them," Price muttered, more rhetorically than as a question.

"No. That's pretty cold, right?"

"Yes, it is. Although, it's what I would have done," Price admitted. "You see, the problem is, you only have maybe ten to twenty seconds during the initial chaos where nobody, not even the attacker, is able to account for everyone."

"Heartless," the Chief of Staff replied.

Price agreed, "Yeah, I'd have taken Townsend with me, because I take care of my friends. But it is a brutal decision by necessity, unfortunately. If you're faced with that kind of firepower, the pistol I have in my pocket is pointless.

The tables and chairs provide no cover at all. If anything,

they're a hindrance. They slow you down and provide zero protection from the bullets.

I hate to say it, but unfortunately, Mary probably chose the only option. Just get the hell out of there as fast as you can. It's every man or woman for them self."

"And in her defence, she probably didn't know most of the people. So, I suspect her actions were more about self-preservation than anything else," the Chief of Staff added in a conciliatory tone.

Price glanced away from the horrific images on the screen and made eye contact with both the Chief and Chief of Staff.

Then he said, "I could have accepted that argument if she had got up and started running. But she didn't.

I think we can all see quite clearly that she anticipated the attack. She had already planned her escape route.

That is the truly brutal part. Because, in the knowledge of what was about to happen, she still just crawled away and left them to die.

So, let's not start misunderstanding what happened in that lovely little restaurant. Let's not delude ourselves gentlemen. She led them to a place she suspected was dangerous and knowingly left them to die - that's the truth of it.

And that's where she and I differ because, whilst she had no choice but to run - I wouldn't lead my friends to their death in the first place."

Once again, nobody spoke for a couple of minutes, until the Chief said, "Where is she Price?"

Price nodded. "I don't know Sir. We kind of lost touch and she didn't reply to my last message. I'll try and track her down."

A slightly suspicious expression appeared on the Chief of Staff's face. Then he said, "Why did you try and contact her at all? You know she's listed as persona non-grata."

Price smiled. "Sex. She has soft hands and lovely..."

The Chief wasn't amused by Price's flippant response and interrupted him by holding up his hand.

"I don't want another massacre. Find her Price. As you just agreed, the way she moved means that she knew the killer the instant she saw him. So, find her, find him and make my problem go away. Clear?"

"Sir," was Price's reply, before muttering, "He's a pro. You can't make out his face properly. He clearly knew where all the cameras were. This guy is very good."

Walking to the exit and without bothering to make eye contact again, the Chief called back, "I don't care Price! This is why we pay you well. Just find him and fix this problem!"

"Of course, Sir," Price called back.

As the Chief vanished out of sight, Price turned to the Chief of Staff. "This is going to be a big problem. Is there really nothing else to go on?"

The Chief of Staff nodded to the operator who switched back to an earlier part of the video - freezing it on Mary's face after having enhanced the image once again, to cater for the poor lighting.

Then he said, "Just your girl. I'm afraid that's all we have. And, I should add, it took us quite a long time to spot that. In fact, it was only when we compared the restaurant seat plan with the body count that we realised one person was unaccounted for."

"And that's it?" Price asked, in total disbelief.

"Find your girl Price. That's all we have for now."

Price was incredulous. His expression said it all. He couldn't believe that their sister service, MI5, or the police had no other evidence.

After a few seconds delay, in an unusually emotional outburst, he said, "This is insane! Just look at how good that killer is. Look at how swiftly he took out what - fifty, sixty - probably not far short of a hundred people?

You do realise what is about to happen? You know we'll all find her at the same time. Just look out for a professional carrying out another massacre.

This has the all the signs of a real pro. He may be a crazy mad nutcase. But I say again, this guy is a pro. You do know that, right? You do realise that he will not stop until he gets what he wants. Whatever the fuck that is!"

Unusually for the Chief of Staff, he also raised his voice to put Price back in his place.

"Find her Price! If you value your position in this firm, you will find her. Fast! Are we absolutely clear on this?"

Price just nodded as he walked out of the room - unaware that only a hundred miles away, Mary was receiving her own equally shocking message.

In her case, however, it was an encrypted message on her mobile phone:

SENDER: HE'S AFTER YOU MY ANGEL :)
MARY: I KNOW. WHERE IS HE?
SENDER: LET'S SEE HOW GOOD YOU REALLY ARE
MARY: YOU CAN FIND HIM. YOU HAVE RESOURCES
MARY: TELL ME WHERE HE IS
SENDER: HAHAHA
MARY: DO YOU WANT ME DEAD?
SENDER: DO YOU WANT TO BE A DEAD ANGEL?
MARY: NO
SENDER: MAYBE YOU ARE NOT THAT GOOD
SENDER: SOON TO BE DEAD
SENDER: HAHAHA
MARY: HELP ME TRACK HIM
SENDER: WHY? THIS IS MORE FUN
MARY: I CAN HELP YOU
SENDER: HE WILL NEVER GIVE UP
SENDER: ITS TOO LATE
MARY: IT ISN'T. TELL ME WHERE HE IS
MARY: PLEASE?
MARY: HELLO?
MARY: ARE YOU THERE?
MARY: BASTARD!!

There was no reply as Mary cursed and threw her phone across the room.

Many miles away Alexei just sat back and laughed.

He enjoyed the mental torture. He enjoyed her suffering. It reinforced his control over her and was payback for all the years she had ordered him around.

8. Black Dolphin

Slavic Stepka sat bolt upright in total silence - covered in sweat and shaking uncontrollably, almost as if he had just received an electric shock.

It was the same nightmare every night - the one he couldn't forget. It seemed to invade his very soul. The traumatic memories of his time at Black Dolphin.

The banging on his cell door - the early morning wake-up call that he became accustomed to at Russia's notorious penal colony number six.

Even though he was no longer there, the memory and the feeling of being there never left his mind - not for a second. The regime, the treatment, the very way of life - bordering on indoctrination.

It wasn't something that you could easily dismiss.

Situated on the edge of Russian Siberia, Black Dolphin dates back to the hard labour camps of the eighteenth century, and is unlike any other prison.

Named after an inmate's sculpture of a black dolphin that sits in front of the main entrance, it's home to seven hundred of the very worst criminals, who between them have killed over four thousand people.

Although, it's not just a place for the mass murderers. It also houses child molesters, terrorists, cannibals and so-called maniacs - as if the other categories were not bad enough.

They are all lifetime inmates by another name - detained in solitary confinement, where they're either asleep or, for sixteen hours each day, not permitted to lay down or sit on their bunks.

Even the exercise yard outside, where they spend ninety minutes each day, is a fully enclosed cage.

Nobody has ever escaped from Black Dolphin. And given the people who are incarcerated there, that's probably a very good thing.

With three steel doors securing each cell - effectively creating another cell within a cell - state-of-the-art motion detection systems, video monitoring and enough security guards to make a visual check on each inmate every fifteen minutes, there really is no hope.

"I'm not going back. I can't go back," he kept thinking.

"Today, she dies. Then I'm free. They let me out to kill her. That's all I have to do, then I can go home."

As he prepared his weapon - once again cleaning and checking the trigger action and the ammunition - his mind kept switching back to his time at Black Dolphin.

All the rules and the routine. Even the soup, which was their only food served four times a day, sent shivers down his spine.

He remembered the other place as well. Although, he couldn't decide if it was better or worse.

Certainly, he had suffered just as much. But that was possibly because of the cold.

Black Eagle - Russia's legendary penal colony number

fifty-six - is a freezing Siberian hell in the middle of a forest larger than Germany, and more than seven hours drive to the nearest city.

It's location alone made escape an impossibility.

Below minus forty in the winter and not much better in the summer. It was not pleasant - the buildings covered in a permanent layer of frozen ice.

Thinking back, he recalled that, whilst the routine wasn't as severe as at Black Dolphin, there was no more hope for the inmates.

Escaping from Black Dolphin was simply impossible.

Escaping from Black Eagle was simply suicide.

It was where the mass murderers ended their lives, with nowhere else to go.

Snapping his brain back to the present, he stood up, his weapon in his hand - exercising his arms and legs so that they were ready.

Looking down at his mobile phone he read the message that was written in his native Russian - making a mental note of the location, before deleting the content.

It was time. It was time to end the nightmare once and for all.

He put his earpieces in and switched on the music - hearing the classical jazz waltz begin, as his mind began to replay events from his childhood.

He remembered all the years spent in an orphanage before he was transferred to his evil foster parents.

Their cruel daily beatings were something he would never forgive or forget - especially when they administered them to his brother or sister.

His only escape from their shouting, arguing and violence was to immerse himself in the same single piece of music.

It had been the only music he had.

A single scratched record - a thirty-year-old disk that just about played on an even more ancient record player.

In the beginning, it made him relax as the notes washed through his brain. He would feel calm and sometimes even content.

But now, so many years later, it just seemed to conjure up feelings of fury and hate - of hurting people in the cruellest ways.

It made him think about torturing them - cutting them in to pieces and watching their blood spurt out as their limbs were severed. Hearing their screams as the life was drained from their bodies.

"They were the ones who taught me how to be like this," he muttered, "Well, now they will pay for what they did and they will learn a lesson from me. This is my time!"

9. Mary

Over the years, Price had learned to trust Mary.

Not the kind of trust you might associate with a normal relationship. Because, he was well aware that she was more than capable of being extremely single-minded, and at times, positively cruel.

It was trust in the sense that, he knew she only ever acted for a reason. She was a professional and nothing was ever random. She always had a plan. Generally, more than one plan.

Thinking back to the carnage he had witnessed on the CCTV footage, Price had to believe that her actions there had been for a reason as well. Although, on the face of it, she appeared to be simply fleeing for her life.

"Let's assume she was fleeing," he considered. "If they are after her then it's entirely possible they could know about our relationship, in which case, it's also possible that they're watching or following me as well - waiting for me to lead them to her."

Price prided himself on his instinct. He always seemed to know if he was being followed - almost as if he had a sixth sense. And certainly, nobody appeared to be following him as he drove home.

That said, "You can't be too careful," he decided.

So, leaving his own mobile phone at home, Price took a train in to central London and bought a cheap phone and a SIM card from a convenience store.

Then, having taken a circuitous route to ensure he was genuinely alone and standing out of sight of any cameras in a crowded pub, he sent a message from and to a pre-agreed email address - a convention he and Mary had memorised many years before in order to keep in touch if, as she put it, "It all goes tits up and we're up shit creek without a paddle."

Price smiled as he finished typing the message.

He kept it short. It simply said:

USUAL PLACE? FRIDAY LUNCH?

Then he hit the send button.

It always made him laugh when she used his slang expressions like, "Tits up."

When he said it, he sounded like a common thug. Whereas she had an inexplicable talent for making foul language sound more like some kind of provocative sexual advance.

"Either that or I'm in love," he concluded, before thinking, "Damn her. Damn her for being so very nice."

Price wasn't expecting a reply any time soon.

Their intention had always been that this would be a method of communication they would use only as a very last resort - when all other options had been tried and disregarded. Consequently, by necessity, it would be something they only monitored occasionally - if only to avoid drawing attention to it.

That said, they also agreed that when it became their only

means of communication, they would monitor it more closely in place of all other mechanisms.

Price still wasn't sure things had got to that point though.

Part of him - his more emotional side - was sceptical that Mary was even involved in the massacre, other than by coincidence. Whilst the more logical side of his brain was certain she was involved - quite possibly implicated in many more ways than had come to light yet.

It didn't take very long for him to find out.

The view of the logical side of his brain was reinforced when, only a few seconds later, the tell-tale ping on the phone indicated that he had a mail.

It read:

HELP! COME NOW! TOO MUCH BUBBLE BATH

Price stared at the message in disbelief.

He didn't know whether he should worry or smile.

The immediacy of her response suggested trouble, whilst the reference to the bubble bath was extremely amusing.

He understood exactly what was meant by her message, even though she hadn't directly given any clue as to her location - something that's key when communicating using media that's not secure.

You have to refer to things that only the sender and receiver will appreciate the relevance of. Preferably things that are so obscure, they cannot be deciphered by even the best analysts with the fastest computers in the world.

And on this occasion, Mary had achieved precisely that.

She had referred to an amusing incident that occurred ten years before. It was one of their first vacations together when they had stayed at a small hotel in the UK's New Forest. A hotel that had a jacuzzi in their suite.

It had been a hugely enjoyable sex-filled experience. Especially, the hilarious moment when they had rather foolishly poured bubble bath in and switched on the jacuzzi pump to circulate the water.

The result was a room full of bubbles and two people who had planned to have a night of sex - but instead spent the evening laughing hysterically.

Most importantly though, it meant that Price, and only Price, knew exactly where she was. The question and the problem at the same time was, how to get there without being followed.

The hotel was only accessible by car and if he drove there, Price knew that he could easily be tracked by a professional team without ever realising it.

Once he had finished the obligatory pint of beer that he had ordered on entering the pub, he ordered a second one - just to make sure it really was as delicious as the first one. Then he laughed, almost literally out loud, as a single word replayed in his mind.

"Bummer."

Around four hours and a couple of extremely cryptic phone calls later, Price smiled as he was waived through the security gate at the entrance to the UK's Special Forces site in Hereford - home to the world renowned Special Air Service.

A tall blonde-haired man was also smiling as he walked

forward to greet Price.

"Price. This is an unexpected pleasure my old friend."

"Bummer!"

Sergeant Shrewsbury, as he was officially known, burst out laughing at the reference to a nickname he'd acquired some years before, as the two men shook hands and patted each other on the back.

"Follow me. Let's get some grub and you can tell me what you need mate."

Price nodded, "Thanks."

Price was convinced his suspicions were correct and that he had been followed to Hereford.

Ordinarily, he expected the smaller country lanes near the SAS site to be empty. But on this occasion, he just never seemed to be alone. Regardless of all the twists and turns and multitude of country lanes, there was always someone there. And, it was never a sports car or something that would catch your eye. No, it was always a really boring car.

Added to which, the last two car number plates were highly questionable.

No intelligence service would use embassy registered cars to follow someone. But SIS, and their sister service MI5, are well aware of this and keep a list of the alternatives their adversaries use. They have the names of, so-called, fake companies that are used to hide the real owner's name. And on this occasion, two had shown up as a match.

This was, most definitely, not just a coincidence.

So, a few hours, and a tour of the Hereford site later, Price's BMW left to head back to London. And as predicted, it picked up a tail almost immediately.

Bummer didn't care though. He drove slowly and carefully. All he needed to do, was avoid a traffic jam.

In a jam, there was a risk that the people following could identify him - specifically, as not being Price. So, he drove steadily and carefully, taking all the small lanes and side roads.

Meanwhile, Price was driven down to the New Forest in an SAS Range Rover - a few hours later, arriving at The Evening Breeze hotel.

It was his favourite hotel in the world, despite the rather strange name that bore no resemblance to the character of the building, which looked more like a country cottage for the rich and famous, than a hotel.

It certainly didn't look like an evening breeze, whatever that was intended to denote.

Despite the strange name, Price always thought about the hotel with affection.

Not just because of the times he and Mary had enjoyed there - although there had been many - but also because of the fantastic service, the food and the suites that each had their own unique character and private jacuzzi.

It was a hotel where under eighteens were not allowed.

It was designed for romance. And romance is what it exuded in every direction.

As he checked in, handing over a credit card under the name of Elliot Smith - a pseudonym that he had used before and had multiple credit cards for - Price smiled inwardly, remembering the truth - the real reason it was his favourite hotel in the world.

It was where he first fell in love with Mary, and she with him.

Whilst waiting for his room key, Price took the opportunity to look around - pleased to see that the hotel had retained its character and appeal.

It had clearly been updated so that nothing looked tired or worn - but at the same time, it wasn't overly modern. It had an aged charm with a reliable modern quality. A perfect mixture of old and new.

It didn't entertain the grotesquely modern - items that were designed to attract art critics who care more about their appearance and hairstyle than the art they are reviewing. Yet, at the same time, there wasn't anything that made you feel you were living in the past.

It certainly wasn't about to start commemorating the last world war, for example.

Price particularly liked the fact that, unlike almost all other hotels in the world, there wasn't really a lobby.

You walked in to what looked more like a large lounge, except for the beautifully carved wooden office desk near the door where someone always sat to provide assistance - in this case, checking Price in.

"There you go Mr Smith," the receptionist spoke, as she handed over Price's room key.

"Would like some help with your bag?"

Price smiled, looking down at his sports bag that only had a couple of changes of clothes.

"Very kind, but I'll be fine," he said. "Thank you again."

Then he walked through the lounge and around a few corners - arriving at his room shortly after.

Price had a well-established routine that he always followed when checking in to a hotel. He always scanned for listening devices and cameras and used a small, but solid, triangular door stop to alert him to people attempting to open the door whilst he was asleep.

Once he was satisfied that the room wasn't bugged, Price showered before making his way to the hotel's bar.

Set in a quiet corner of the large lounge, it's wooden bar top and oak timber beams fitted perfectly in to the traditional country cottage character of the building.

Price had no idea what name Mary had used at the hotel, and he was certainly not about to risk sending her a message. So, he just sat quietly and sipped at his drink - pleasantly surprised by a cool breeze that took the edge off what had been an unusually warm day for the time of year.

He was just thinking about the breeze and wondering if that had contributed to the owner's unusual choice of name for the hotel, when he was disturbed.

The familiar soft Asian voice whispered in his ear - so close that he could feel the breath.

"I think you're putting on weight you know."

Price smiled as he turned and quietly replied, "I'm not getting enough sex. That's the problem."

Mary looked at Price with what he always described as her evil smile - thinking, "This will be trouble!"

"Fuck me here. Right now. I dare you. Rip my clothes off and take me from behind on the bar."

Price smiled but didn't reply. Instead, he just looked into Mary's eyes. The eyes that always seemed to captivate him.

For some reason, they had an almost hypnotic quality which attracted him, although he could never really describe why.

He knew she was able to switch on her expressions at will, to manipulate his brain. And most of the time he didn't care. He just let himself fall for her beauty and become mesmerized.

Not this time though. People had died. A friend in the Firm, as he always referred to SIS, had died. So, after a few seconds, Price shook his head and forced his brain to block out the desire.

"Tell me what's going on. Why am I here?"

Mary's expression and mood changed in an instant.

"You damned Brits. Why do you insist on being so business like? Why can't we have a conversation for a few minutes before we discuss work?"

Price picked up his drink and took a sip before saying, "You know it's wonderful to see you again. But I think we know each other well enough that we don't need to play out that scene every time we meet."

Mary nodded in agreement as Price continued, "I was just wondering why I'm here. Is it something you did, something your country did or something someone else did to you?"

"It was me, not my country or anyone else!"

Price's expression turned to a mixture of curiosity and concern as he slowly asked, "Exactly what have you done?"

"It's very bad and more than a bit complicated darling."

"Is anything ever straightforward with you?"

"I could say the same to you darling, and your country. After all, look at all the arguing over your 5G network."

Price smiled in agreement, "Yes, I think I'm with you on that one. We do appear to have developed a certain paranoia regarding anything Chinese."

"I think the general public never really understood the real motives darling."

"True. The British public and the press didn't want your 5G because everyone was panicking about you trying to hack our networks. What they forgot was, we need your 5G systems so we can learn how to hack yours!"

Mary burst out laughing as she said, "That's so true. Your people think they are saints, when in reality."

Price finished the sentence for her, "We are all the same in the end. You spy on us, we spy on you. We all get very judgmental, but in reality, we are all as good or as bad as each other."

After another drink, Price stopped smiling. He just stared in to the eyes he loved and said, "Stop changing the subject and tell me why. Why am I here? And why were you in that restaurant? What have you done that's caused this?"

Mary leaned closer, whispering so that she could not be heard by anyone else, and said, "I'm being hunted like prey. It's just a matter of time Price. I'm afraid it's serious this time. You remember the Russian agent who I told you was working for me. Alexei?"

"Yes of course I remember him. He saved my life in Syria. I am somewhat in his debt."

"Yes, well. It's not that simple because."

Price stopped Mary mid-sentence - jamming his hand over her mouth.

As they made eye contact, Price whispered, "I can hear a worrying sound."

Without speaking, Mary's eyes asked what he was referring to.

"I can hear classical music. To be specific, it's a waltz! We're in trouble. Get ready to move."

Suddenly the lights went out.

Price grabbed Mary's arm as he started to guide her towards the exit, where he knew they would benefit from the streetlights outside - clearly visible in the distance, despite the darkness inside the building.

Having pushed Price's hand away, Mary's voice changed as they hurried across the room. Her soft smooth tone completely gone - only to be replaced by another tone - one that was harsh and accusing.

"You fool. You were followed here."

"No. That's not possible. I."

Price was about to say that he took every precaution. However, before he could finish the sentence, a large dark figure appeared by the door ahead of them.

To Price's horror, Mary shook herself free of his grip and darted to their left - he presumed towards another exit that he wasn't aware of.

Once again, she had clearly planned her escape route.

He wanted to follow, but couldn't see - she had run in to a corner of the room that was now completely shrouded in darkness.

Price hesitated for a second.

He recognised the figure before him from the Italian restaurant massacre. The stature of the man and the coat.

Even in the poor lighting he had a certain presence. He was a most capable and brutal killer - that was for sure.

As the man pulled back his coat and withdrew a weapon, Price suddenly remembered there was a corridor next to the bar. He couldn't see it, but he knew it was there from past visits - and he knew there was an exit at the end of it. It opened to the rear garden. So, he turned and sprinted in to the darkness, just as the intruder opened fire.

The thuds of the suppressed bullets seemed to echo around the room as Price fled - his arm raised in front of his face, in case he ran in to something in the poor lighting.

Behind him, he could hear the screams as lives were ruthlessly cut short. The bullets tearing organs apart and once again turning an idyllic scene in to carnage.

Price could also hear the killer moving around as the bullets ricocheted off the hotel's walls - the direction of the sound giving him a clue as to the direction he was moving.

Looking at one of the hotel corridors, it occurred to Price that, if it was Mary the killer was after, he would inevitably kill everyone in the hotel whilst searching for her.

He had to try and do something. So, he hit the fire alarm. At least that way people could run, rather than just wait in their rooms to be murdered.

At the back of the hotel by a fire door, Price stood guard with his gun in his hand, and watched as guests, reacting to the fire alarm, sprinted out in to a field.

After a few minutes, judging that anyone who was going to leave had already left, Price very carefully made his way back in to the building - searching the corridors as he headed back towards the lounge, intent on trying to surprise the killer.

Instead, however, all he found were dead bodies and mass devastation.

"At least a few people made it out," Price thought, as he pocketed his gun and made a call to the emergency services.

A conversation with the Chief later the same evening

confirmed that twenty-four innocent people were now dead. It was a combination of locals, tourists and hotel staff.

As before, the body count included men, women and children. There was gunfire followed by the gruesome cutting of people's limbs - in some cases even slicing their head in two.

The power and strength of the attacker was clear.

Then as before, he had vanished without a trace - just a burning wreck of a stolen car as evidence. Nothing of use to the police forensic department.

To add to Price's dismay, he was convinced that he had been followed back to his apartment.

He didn't have any real evidence. However, as he related to the Chief, "Something didn't feel right Sir. I'm sure I was being watched the entire time."

"Maybe you were. He found you somehow. Is there anything else to go on?"

Price thought back, "Just one thing Sir. The last thing Mary said before the lights went out and we made our escape, was something about Alexei. You know, the Russian agent that I met in Syria?"

Price could hear the Chief typing on a computer keyboard as he said, "Really. Now that is interesting. Give me a second if you would please."

Then a few moments later there was shouting. The Chief had picked up his other phone and was bellowing at someone with a most uncharacteristic level of aggression.

Price just waited until the Chief returned - this time reverting to his calm voice. He said, referring to the UK's Security Service, MI5, "Five have just confirmed that Alexei slipped in to the country on a false passport a few weeks back. Could it have been him?"

Price closed his eyes, remembering the image of the man who had saved his life in Syria - comparing him with the dark the figure in the hotel.

They were both very tall, imposing and noticeably strong men. But, he couldn't be sure they were they the same man. They both moved liked military men with ruthless precision and efficiency. But then again, that could describe anyone who had worked in the special forces.

"I don't know Sir. It was impossible to tell in the dark. They're the same build I guess, as are a million others. He has to be a suspect though. It has to be more than a coincidence."

"I agree. I don't believe she said that by chance, any more than you do."

Price paused before replying - something the Chief picked up on immediately. "What else is there Price?"

"He had time Sir."

"What do you mean?"

"He could easily have taken me out Sir. He had ample time to take the shot."

"Are you sure?"

"Yes. He waited until I ran and then he started firing from the opposite direction. He let me go. In his position, I would not have hesitated."

"You're certain?"

"If it had been me standing where he was, I would not be here today. Of that, I am absolutely certain Sir. Whoever he is, he hesitated. I'm telling you Sir, if the situation was reversed, I promise you we would not be speaking."

"So, you think it could have been Alexei then? Maybe he recognised you. Maybe your relationship, or rather history is probably a better way of putting it, saved your life?"

"If it's him, then I'd say yes Sir. If it's not, then maybe it's someone else who recognised me and wasn't after me. I honestly don't know, other than he definitely hesitated."

"That's quite an interesting perspective since he killed everyone else regardless of who they were."

"Or he needed to keep me alive to find her. That's always a possibility Sir."

The Chief agreed, "Yes, I can see that. That could be a plausible explanation. Or maybe it was something as simple as the gun jammed."

"It didn't Sir. I know what I saw."

"Then you got lucky Price!"

"Yes, I most certainly did," Price conceded, before asking, "You said Alexei had a false passport Sir. What type of false passport are we talking about, if you know what I mean?"

The Chief understood exactly what Price was referring to.

"It was an official one. Five seemed pretty certain of that. This wasn't some cheap counterfeit. The only reason it got flagged was because of face recognition. Five reckon he was most likely inserted officially by their security services, presumably with a task to do."

"I don't believe they'd task him with mass murder Sir. The FSB don't engage in that kind of thing."

The Chief agreed, "No Price. I don't think so either. Unless he's here for a purpose and has gone off the rails. Get some sleep. We'll try and track him down."

The following morning, just ten miles away, Mary slept in a small hotel room in central London - a few blocks away from London's Edgeware Road, where many old town houses have been converted for commercial use.

Some, are small establishments that offer a low-cost alternative to tourists not wishing to pay the premium rates charged by the large four and five-star hotel chains.

Whilst others offer the less-reputable, but arguably more honest, services that are frequently charged by the hour.

It was the latter type of establishment where Mary had rented a room - in her case for the entire night.

She wasn't interested in the services they offered. She just needed a place to sleep. Somewhere they didn't ask too many questions. Although, she noted that the downside of that kind of establishment was the noise.

Throughout the night she heard doors being opened and slammed shut again, and quite a lot of screaming and shouting - sometimes from joy, but mostly she presumed, from anger and disappointment.

Consequently, it was the early hours of the morning before her body truly relaxed and she descended in to deep sleep - only to be disturbed all too soon.

The buzz of her mobile phone indicated she had a new message.

Brushing the sleep from her eyes, Mary focused as she opened the message - recognising her secret call-sign.

However, she was angry.

She was angry, tired and bitter at being contacted again. Especially after the events of the previous evening.

SENDER: MORNING ANGEL :)
MARY: I DID WHAT YOU ASKED
MARY: VITALY IS DEAD
MARY: EITHER HELP ME OR LEAVE ME ALONE!!!!
SENDER: IT'S ALL CHANGED NOW ANGEL
SENDER: WE NEED TO MEET
MARY: NO WAY
MARY: I DID WHAT YOU ASKED
MARY: LEAVE ME ALONE
SENDER: YOU WILL REGRET THIS ANGEL
MARY: EITHER TELL ME WHERE HE IS OR GO TO HELL
SENDER: WE NEED TO MEET
MARY: GO TO HELL!!
SENDER: I'LL FIND YOU ANYWAY
SENDER: I'LL FOLLOW YOUR BOYFRIEND AND THEN TELL HIM AGAIN
MARY: HE DOESN'T KNOW WHERE I AM
SENDER: I'M SURE YOU'LL CALL HIM
MARY: GO TO HELL!!!!

Before the sender could reply, Mary switched off her phone and packed her bags.

"I just have to keep moving," she told herself. "It's my only chance of survival."

At around the same time, Price was speaking to the Chief of Staff at SIS headquarters in Vauxhall Cross, when the phone rang. It was the UK's Government Communication Headquarters, otherwise known as GCHQ.

The Chief of Staff took the call, which lasted a few minutes.

Price could only hear one side of the conversation, so instead of trying to guess what they were saying, he made himself a coffee. He was just adding the milk when the Chief of Staff walked in to the kitchen.

"That was GCHQ. Mary received a message in central London a few moments ago. They know it was her because, sadly, very few other mobiles made it out of the New Forest alive last night."

Price couldn't help feeling a certain sense of guilt. Should he have stopped and made a fight out of it? He knew he would have been totally out-gunned and wouldn't have survived. But it may have given a few more people time to escape. Maybe he could have prevented quite so much carnage - which was, after all, his job.

The Chief of Staff sensed Price's mind had drifted, so he raised his voice to ensure he was heard.

"Price! We've tracked the message. They're working on decrypting it. The first part doesn't seem to be useful. It was something about leave me alone. But it does give us a number to monitor, and, for now at least, a location."

Price looked up from his coffee - evidently still deep in

thought.

"She'll be gone by the time we get there. She'll know we picked it up. She'll move Sir."

The Chief of Staff nodded agreement. "GCHQ said the phone had been switched off, so I'm sure you're right. I'd bet she'll switch it on again at some point though. If only to check for messages from you."

"I already tried to get in touch via email Sir. There's been no reply as yet. I'll let you know if she does message me."

"Do you think Alexei would turn on her? I thought you said he worked for her, correct? "

"She said he did. But would he turn on her? I guess it depends on what she is demanding Sir. Everyone has their limit, right? You can only push people so far in this world before they break. Especially people like Alexei. I doubt he's the easiest person to get on with. I should imagine he's quite a difficult and volatile character."

"OK, well GCHQ will track the phone as soon as it's switched on again. Once it stays in one place long enough to triangulate an exact location, we'll let you know."

"What about the messenger? The person sending her the messages. Any idea who that was or where they were?"

The Chief of Staff nodded no.

"It was routed via servers around the world - half of whom probably were not even aware they were sending it."

"So, it's a professional job then."

"Very much so. And, not wishing to make your day any

worse, I'm afraid there's some other news you need to be aware of."

Price didn't reply - he just waited for the Chief of Staff to continue.

"Do you remember the name Slavic Stepka?"

Price recognised the name, but couldn't recollect details from the file.

"Sorry Sir. Let me check the file."

"It's OK. Here's the thirty second version, which you'll need, because apparently he's managed to slip past border security - although, we don't know where and we don't even know when."

"What the hell! How can that be Sir?"

The Chief of Staff ignored Price's rather loud outburst and continued speaking.

"Slavic Stepka is an extremely brutal and professional killer."

"That part I do remember," Price interrupted.

"He may be after the killer in black - we don't know yet. If the killer is Alexei, then that would make sense because the Russians wouldn't want a rogue agent out there any more than we do. A rogue agent could undermine the effectiveness of their real operatives."

"In danger of making them look like a bunch of fucking amateurs - excuse my French Sir."

"Indeed, it would. And as you know, amateurs they're most certainly not."

"How the hell did he get in? He's well known to us."

"We're not sure. As you know, Alexei's entry was flagged because of the face recognition software we have installed across the country and at all the borders and ports.

Slavic Stepka, however, was only flagged when he entered a strip club in central London, that just happens to be run by a friend of the firm."

"His insertion was even more discrete than Alexei's then. I'm not sure what to make of that."

The Chief of Staff agreed, "Either he's here officially and they are really serious about not wanting us to know, or he's gone rogue. Or maybe Alexei's insertion was some kind of deliberate misdirection. At this point, we just don't know. It's all speculation."

Price smiled, "You said a strip club run by a friend of the firm. You don't mean?"

"Yes. It was your old buddy from the Paras, Chas."

Whilst laughing, Price replied, "He lets you tap in to the dodgy CCTV cameras in his seedy little club?"

"Yes. And not just his cameras. We've fitted more than just one or two of our own, in return for which we make some charitable donations to him. So, before you say it, yes! We pay him to record videos of girls taking their clothes off. Although, it's the people they take them off for that we are really watching - not the girls themselves."

Price laughed. "Cheeky bastard. And very nice work if you can get it. What else do we know about Stepka?"

Glancing down at his notes, the Chief of Staff continued, "Well, he grew up in Bratislava with a Russian father, Slovakian mother. He was recruited by the Russian FSB after a spell in the army and their Spetsnaz. He made a bit of cash for a few years as one if their top specialists."

"Specialists?"

"Like you Price. He did the most dangerous and dirty work, and was reasonably well paid for it. We thought he had retired a few years back. He rather mysteriously vanished for no apparent reason. Then, equally mysteriously, a year or so ago, he reappeared again.

This time, however, he seemed to have developed an interest in the arms smuggling business. Now he looks to be focusing on that - aside from the occasional one-off jobs as hired help."

"So, basically," Price interrupted, "He's an overpaid killer and now just does it for fun, right?"

"Not exactly. He is hired help. But as I say, these days he seems to be extremely good at discretely transporting arms internationally. He's certainly not the brains behind it. Of that, we are quite certain. But, he's moved a shit-load of kit - including a few shipments for us I might add. I'm ashamed to admit it. But he has."

"Sir, for fuck sake. Don't we have any standards?"

The Chief of Staff didn't reply, so Price continued, "Is there anything else I should know? Because, if you're right and he is here to get the killer in black, I'm bound to bump in to him - since I'm after the same guy."

"Sadly, yes. You need to ask your friend Chas. Don't worry, we'll keep an eye on the mobile phone and let you know if Mary shows up."

Price was suspicious - it was unlike the Chief of Staff to evade questions.

"What aren't you telling me Sir?"

The Chief of Staff didn't immediately reply, so Price asked the question again - but this time, somewhat more assertively.

"What's going on Sir? Why the secrecy? It's a perfectly reasonable question. What other information do we have on this guy?"

The Chief of Staff paused for thought - evidently unsure how to reply.

After a few moments where neither man spoke, he eventually said, "Price, Slavic Stepka is not a person you would ever want to meet. My best advice to you as a colleague and, more importantly, as your friend, is to try and avoid him at all costs."

"Why? Just tell me why? I've met unpleasant people before Sir."

"Price."

"No Sir! This is unacceptable! I'm going out there and could be facing a dangerous man. What is going on?"

Price was about to speak again when the Chief of Staff interrupted.

"Speak to your friend Price. Please, just speak to him and you'll understand what I'm saying and what I'm not saying."

"Why?"

"He's met this guy face-to-face. Just speak to him. Please. I'm not just saying this as a work colleague. I promise you, I'm saying this as your friend Price."

Price didn't reply.

However, after a few seconds as Price was walking away, the Chief of Staff, in an unusually sombre tone, added, "Price?"

Price glanced back, "Sir?"

"Please, be careful my friend. Please. Please be very careful."

Price just nodded and walked off.

10. Slavic Stepka

Price couldn't help smiling as he walked down the small lane in London's Soho district - seeing a scantily clad woman standing outside the door to the club that his long-time friend from the Parachute Regiment, Chas, owned and managed.

"This is not a bad life," he thought - reminding himself that Chas was getting paid for gathering intelligence at the same time as running a strip club.

Whilst some people might think that it's a waste of SIS money to monitor these establishments, Price new better. The so-called honey-trap was, and always will be, one of the great ways to recruit spies and collect information.

Nobody wants to get caught metaphorically, or in many cases literally, with their trousers down.

As soon as Price reached the club's entrance, the woman walked towards him, whilst for his part, he just stared at her breasts. He couldn't help it and made no apology for the fact. Not only were they huge, they were accentuated by a push-up bra that was clearly there to deliberately attract attention - something it was undeniably achieving

"Huge made bigger," was the thought that crossed Price's mind, as he ignored what she was saying, choosing instead to interrupt her with, "I'm here to see Chas please. Possibly Charles or maybe even Charlie, depending on what he's calling himself this week?"

He had intended it to be a light-hearted remark.

Sadly, however, it was most certainly not received as such.

Her expression changed in an instant.

The hostility was obvious on her face as she said, "Who are you and what the fuck do you want?" - her East European accent emphasising the f-word and, if anything, making it even more offensive than it would normally be.

"Price. Please tell him it's Price."

Without breaking eye contact, the woman screamed out a name that Price didn't quite catch. However, when one of the largest and most imposing men he'd ever seen, walked out, Price realised what she had actually done. She had called a bouncer. A bouncer who was armed to the teeth, judging by the bulge under his jacket.

Knowing that she now had the upper hand, the woman began to smile. A rather smug smile Price observed - whilst recognizing that she was right to be smug - the bouncer was truly enormous.

With a calm voice, Price said, "Charles is a friend. I just wanted to say hi."

The bouncer who, up to this point hadn't said a word, asked, "Are you expected?"

"No."

"Get lost then."

Price nodded as he pointed to the pocket where his mobile phone was stowed, and said, "I'll phone him, OK?"

Once again, the bouncer didn't speak. So, Price took that to be agreement and, very carefully removed his mobile phone from his pocket.

The last thing he needed was to be shot for trying to make a phone call.

Chas answered pretty much immediately. "Price, great to hear from you mate. How are you?"

"I'm mostly OK, but about to get the shit kicked out of me, if not worse. Please could you tell your security that I'm a friend."

A door at the end of the corridor behind the security guard opened - revealing itself for the first time. Up to that point it had been hidden by a combination of the low-level lighting and the matt black walls, floor and ceiling.

Chas walked out, his mobile in his hand, and shouted, "Freddy, he's a mate. It's fine."

The bouncer stepped to one side so that Price could enter. Whilst for his part, Price gave a polite nod combined with a respectful, "Thank you."

The bouncer nodded back as Price met Chas and they patted each other on the back.

"Freddy is my head of security."

Price looked back and made eye contact with Freddy as he said, "I can see why. He scared the crap out of me for a second there."

The bouncer acknowledged Price's remarks with the very slightest, almost imperceptible smile, before reverting to his intimidating professional stance.

As Price sat down in Chas's apartment, watching his old friend make a coffee, Chas spoke first.

"I was expecting you actually. I received an email from your boss. Understand you need some information mate, but he wouldn't say what it was about."

"Yeah. Anything you know about Slavic Stepka, if that name means anything to you?"

Chas hesitated momentarily. Then, without looking up, continued pouring the coffee as he said, "What do you want with that sick fuck?"

Price was a little surprised by the response. However, undeterred he said, "They told me you could tell me more about him. He might be involved in a case I'm working on."

Chas handed Price his coffee before sitting down.

"You saw Freddy, right? You saw what he's like?"

Price nodded - aware that it was more of a rhetorical question than anything else.

"I have two more the same size. When Stepka came in here and tried to rape one of my ladies, it took all four of us to get him out. I was a second away from sticking a bullet in his head mate."

Price was about to speak, but Chas interrupted, "It was the girl out there actually. Doorknob."

"Doorknob?"

"Yeah. It's just a stupid nickname. The joke is, she's a

doorknob because everyone's had a turn."

Price laughed. He was half tempted to remark that she must have benefited from the poor lighting - but decided it probably wasn't very helpful on this occasion.

Chas continued, "She does what she does willingly. I don't force her to do anything with the punters. She gets paid to get guys through the door. If she wants to mess around with them for extra tips, that's up to her. I couldn't give a shit. Ninety-five percent of her cash comes from me, and she gets that regardless of what she does with them."

"Then?"

"Then he turned up, punched her in the face, ripped off half her clothes and tried to screw her on the floor of the fucking bar mate!"

Price was speechless - his eyes widened in surprise, as he wondered what motivated people to do that kind of thing anywhere - let alone in a public place.

"There's videos of him with young girls as well. I had him followed for your boss."

Price's voice changed to a more depressed tone as he reluctantly asked, "How young?"

"Too fucking young. Single digits mate."

Price cringed. Now he knew why the Chief of Staff had been reluctant to speak about Slavic Stepka. As a father of three young daughters, it must have been even more disturbing for him.

"So, he's one of those, is he? We need to get rid of him."

"Yes mate, we do. He makes them call him names. Then

he makes them beg him to do things to them. Gets them to say, Daddy do this, do that, and the like. You don't want to know mate. I'm telling you. Slavic Stepka is one seriously sick fucked up bastard!"

"Has he come back?" Price asked, wondering if he'd get an opportunity to meet the man face-to-face.

"No. And if he does, I can assure you, he won't be walking out alive. Everyone's got his picture. I shared it with all the bouncers in the neighbourhood. First one to cap him gets free blow jobs off Doorknob for a year."

Price laughed. "That's a valuable commodity you have there. People pay good money for that kind of thing."

Chas gave a half-smile - a polite smile that he clearly didn't really mean - put on purely to acknowledge the joke.

Price didn't speak. He just sipped his coffee whilst he looked across the room at his old friend - recognizing that Slavic Stepka had clearly made quite an impression.

"Price, I'm telling you. I know what you're capable of, but you don't want to meet him. Stay clear mate. That guy is strong, huge and fucked up. And, rumour has it, the Russians thought so as well and locked him up for a couple of years."

"Yeah, the Chief said he went missing for a while," Price acknowledged.

"Yeah well, now you know why."

"I wonder why they let him out?"

"I heard it was for some special job. Something to do with

that nerve gas in London. That's all I know mate."

Price still thought it was strange that he'd been granted his freedom. Whilst he didn't necessarily agree with Russian politics or their political system - he was certain they agreed on how to treat people like Slavic Stepka.

However, putting that thought to one side, he asked, "Have you got any CCTV footage that I could get a look at? Not the attack please. I've no desire to see that. I just want to get a view of the man because, whilst I appreciate your advice, I have a feeling our paths may cross."

Chas picked up his mobile phone, connected to his security system and played a video for Price.

Not surprisingly, it was taken at night, so it was difficult to make out any real features. Added to which, the little he could make out was repeatedly washed out by intermittent flashes from neon lights that were advertising girls and shows in nearby bars and clubs.

Seeing that Price was struggling to make out details, Chas switched to a recording from the night vision cameras.

It certainly provided a clearer view to track the man's movements - but even then, the grey images were not something you could readily use to try and get a measure of the man.

One thing was for sure though. By the way he walked down the street and entered the club, Slavic Stepka had clearly been extremely drunk that night.

Price initially wondered why they let him in. Then he thought, "Actually, that's obvious. After all, why would anyone go to a bar like that when they're sober? It's the way these types of establishment operate. If you don't let the drunks in you'll have no customers."

"When was this?" he asked.

"Couple of weeks ago I guess. All my security guys have been armed to the teeth ever since."

"I can see that. Bit excessive don't you think," Price replied. "This is central London after all. There's an army of cops only minutes away. Not to mention the SAS counter terrorism team just a few hundred yards from Buckingham Palace. You know that as well as anyone."

Chas was in no mood for being lectured.

"When we chucked him out, he swore he would come back and get his revenge. He was shouting murder, torture, sexual abuse and all sorts of other shit!"

"Chas. We've all shouted crap over the years. He was drunk."

Chas made eye contact with Price as he said, "I'm telling you mate - he meant it. I could see it in his eyes. I even ran back to the office and picked up my gun. Sadly, by the time I got back he'd done a runner."

"Wow that is seriously messed up. You were actually going to shoot him for real?"

"Yeah, I was. So, take my advice and don't bump in to him mate. And if you do, just shoot the fucker in the face."

Price was about to reply when his phone vibrated. It was SIS, so he answered, "This is Price."

The Chief of Staff's voice was unmistakable.

"GCHQ have located your girl's phone. She's in a small

holiday home down in Somerset. Basically, she is hiding out in the middle of nowhere."

"Is she on her own?"

"Yes. For the moment. Aside from the SAS guy that we have watching her."

"Who?"

"Shrewsbury. You know him, right?"

"Yes. Tell him I'm on my way would you."

"OK. I'm sending you her exact location now."

Chas gave Price a quizzical look, as if to ask what had happened.

"This is all linked to Mary."

Chas laughed, but before he could speak Price continued, "She appears to be on the run for some unknown reason and GCHQ have managed to locate her. So, thanks for the coffee mate and the briefing on Stepka. But, sadly I need to go."

"Where? Where is she?"

"Somerset."

Chas switched off his coffee machine, picked up his wallet and car keys, then said, "I can't hang around to support you, but I can run you down there in the Porsche if you like."

"Your pimp waggon?"

As they walked out of Chas's apartment to the underground garage where he stored his car, he had to admit, the bright red leather seats inside his black sports car were not exactly subtle. But as he commented, "They're comfortable, I like them, so actually, I really don't give a shit what everybody else thinks."

For his part, Price didn't take convincing - graciously accepting the offer and promising to re-pay the favour in beers.

An hour or so later, they were making their way down the UK's legendary A303 trunk road - the subject of many discussions over the years, along with a few rock songs.

Chas asked, "Is she being watched? I mean, you don't want to arrive and find she's left."

"Yeah, an SAS guy is watching her."

"Oh who? Anyone I know?"

"Not sure you know him. Bummer?"

Chas laughed as he said, "Ah, Shrewsbury. Yeah, I've heard of him. I still don't know how he got the nickname though."

"Really? I shall explain then."

A nod in reply, signalled that he should.

"It was quite a few years ago. Shrew and me were supporting an operation to extract some Foreign Office officials who'd managed to get caught up in local militia disturbances in Africa - Somalia to be specific - towards the south of Mogadishu if I remember rightly."

Chas laughed, "Wasn't that the most dangerous city in the world at one point?"

"Yeah, it's getting better now, but it's still quite rough. It's the shanty towns that are the real problem. They're made up of hundreds of rundown buildings - some that bare a greater resemblance to cardboard boxes than houses, to be honest. And in some cases, they're separated by only a few feet, creating what looks like a maze.

Aside from the health issues of living in such close proximity to each other, they're perfect for criminals. They run out of a dark alleyway, kill someone - or if the victim is lucky, just take their money - and vanish again in to the darkness."

"Sounds like a bundle of fun."

"As I say, it's still dangerous, but it is getting better," Price repeated. "It's certainly nowhere near as bad as it used to be, which is why the Foreign Office and UN officials were there. They were helping to improve the living conditions and provide humanitarian aid for the less fortunate.

We were told to just watch and only intervene if they were threatened. So, we turned up dressed like a couple of poor backpackers, in an attempt to avoid standing out, and just hung around mixing with the locals.

Imagine lots of battle-scarred single and two-story stone buildings in various states of repair - worryingly close to the a nearby shanty town.

Our people were safely hiding inside one of the more substantial concrete buildings when their transport arrived. Basically, half a dozen armoured 4X4's that were to take them back to the airport.

To be honest, it looked like it was going to be a straight-forward pick-up. But, as soon as the car doors opened, a crowd of onlookers moved towards them - more out of curiosity than anything else I suspect. Then we heard some shouting and then gunfire.

Shrew and I turned to see two armed men who were firing directly in to the crowd.

They were maniacs. At one point, they were in the middle of a large group of people and were still trying to fire their weapons at the UN team.

There was no way the UN bodyguards or Shrew and I could return fire. Our shots would have passed straight through them and taken out women and children behind them. It would have been a massacre."

"Hand to hand combat it is then." Chas added.

"Pretty much. We drew our knives and I shouted that the one on the left was mine. Shrew went for the other one."

"I think I'd be quite worried in that situation. You can't help thinking that half the crowd could be their buddies. What if they all turned on you?"

Price agreed, "If that had happened, we wouldn't have stood a chance in hell. It would have been carnage. As it turned out though, I got lucky and caught the guy side-on. My knife plunged in to his neck before he knew what had hit him. Then I used it to drag him to the floor and game over."

"And Shrew? "

"Shrew wasn't quite so lucky. The other guy turned at the last second and saw him."

"Oh dear."

"Yeah. He managed to fling himself to the side so that Shrew's knife missed. But, that also meant he was slightly off balance. So, with a lunge forward, Shrew knocked the guy down - unfortunately, losing his grip on his knife in the process.

The guy tried to turn, still gripping his gun - but Shrew was ready for him and, after a bit of a struggle, managed to disarm him before he could do any more damage. In doing that, however, Shrew lost his grip on the guy's arm."

"I hope the guy didn't have another weapon."

"Luckily no. But he did manage to scramble to his feet and start to run."

"OK, but he can't have got far. At such close range, why not shoot him in the leg or something," Chas interrupted. "That's what I'd have done."

Price started to laugh, "If it had been me, I'd have shot him with his own gun, that was now lying on the ground. As you say, one to the leg at such close quarters would have stopped him without risking anyone else. However, Shrew didn't."

"What? Why not? Is he nuts?"

"Who knows. For a reason that he still can't explain to this day, he ignored the gun and picked up his knife. Then, he dived after him. It was a proper rugby tackle. He claims he had been planning to stab him in the leg."

"I'm guessing you're about to say, but?"

"But he missed. The guy must have caught his foot on something - maybe a rock I guess, who knows. Anyway, whatever it was it slowed the guy down."

"Don't tell me he stabbed the guy's arse?"

"Worse. The guy slipped and started to fall forward, just as Shrew lunged forward with the knife. As a result, it went straight up the guy's arse."

Chas burst out laughing, "What?"

"Yeah, it went up the crack of his arse, forwards, out the front and cut his knob in two."

"Ouch!"

"Slowed the guy down," Price joked.

"I'm sure it did," Chas replied. "That would definitely bring tears to your eyes."

"Anyway, the joke was that he'd bummed the guy. Hence, Bummer it's been ever since."

Chas carried on laughing, even as he asked, "Just out of curiosity, does he care that's his nickname?"

Price looked across at Chas. "No of course not. Of all the people in The Regiment, he couldn't care less about stuff like that. He finds it funny. And when he's drunk in bars and clubs, that's how he introduces himself to girls."

Chas laughed again, "And how does that work out?"

"Well it doesn't of course. It freaks them out. They think he's some kind of maniac. It's quite funny to watch though."

As the laughing subsided, Chas's mind switched back to their more immediate situation.

He asked, "More importantly. Why are we looking for your girl? Why is she on the run? And what has she got to do with Slavic Stepka?"

"I don't know. At least, I don't know yet. All I do know is, someone is trying to kill her. And by coincidence, two Russian's arrived in the country not so long ago. Slavic Stepka and another guy you may not know, named Alexei."

Chas nodded, "No I don't know the other guy. What's he like?"

"He's another huge special forces guy. Hard as nails."

"And we think the killer is one of them?" Chas asked.

"Not for sure. But it's a bit of a coincidence don't you think? "Yeah."

"Plus," Price continued, "When I last spoke to Mary, she mentioned Alexei's name. So, we're wondering if maybe Stepka is here to find him. But it's just guesswork - it could easily be the other way round."

Neither man spoke for a while as the journey continued. Until Price, looking down at his mobile and said, "We're nearly there."

Then he messaged Bummer - only to be told that Mary had gone for a walk and was at that moment sitting in a nearby café. Bummer expected her to return later, as she'd left all her belongings behind.

Price was about to ask what she was doing in the café, as he wanted to know if she was meeting someone. However, before he could ask, Bummer messaged back that she was alone and appeared to be using her mobile phone.

Price smiled to himself.

Whilst he believed Bummer, he didn't believe Mary was just using her phone. He was sure that her real motivation would have been to see if she was being observed.

Knowing her as he did, he was sure she would have spotted Bummer.

So, to avoid detection himself, Price thanked his friend and jumped out of the car a mile away, before cautiously making his way across country.

The landscape was relatively flat and mostly wooded, with the ground covered in leaves as is typical of a British autumn.

As Price cautiously made his way towards the country cottage - a small two-story grey stone building that sat on the bank of a small river.

He was relieved to be able to use the trees to stay out of sight, whilst constantly scanning the horizon with his infrared monocular - not dissimilar to the device he knew Mary used in similar circumstances.

No heat sources appeared in the viewfinder, even as he approached to within a few hundred yards of the cottage.

Looking at it from a distance, he had to admit, it was a charming building, exactly as Bummer had described it - a quaint country home next to a fast-flowing river.

Suddenly, Price's phone buzzed.

BUMMER: SHE'S GONE
PRICE: WHERE?

BUMMER: SHE WENT TO THE BATHROOM
PRICE: YOU KNOB
BUMMER: SORRY BE CAREFUL PLS
PRICE: OK
BUMMER: I WILL FIND HER

Price cursed, thinking, "That is most unlikely. She'll be gone unless she wants you to find her."

He knew that Bummer was an outstanding soldier - a true hero in a fight. Nobody had more courage, determination, stamina and tenacity. But this called for more subtle skills.

"He'll pay for that mistake in beer," Price decided, just as another message caused his phone to buzz.

He fully expected it to be Bummer again - but it wasn't.

MARY: GOT YOU ON INFRARED
MARY: HAHAHA
MARY: COME TO THE COTTAGE
PRICE: SHOW UR FACE FIRST
MARY: I HAVE BEER
PRICE: WHY DIDN'T YOU SAY BEFORE?
PRICE: THAT CHANGES EVERYTHING
MARY: I THOUGHT IT MIGHT
PRICE: YOU CALLING ME SHALLOW?
MARY: OBVIOUSLY!
MARY: WHY? IS THAT A PROBLEM?

Reading Mary's text, Price couldn't help laughing as he replied.

PRICE: OF COURSE NOT. I WAS JUST CHECKING

Price stepped out from behind a tree, where he had been watching the cottage from a distance - only to see Mary appear by the building's entrance.

She had evidently been hiding behind a stone wall which had obscured her from detection as an infrared signature when Price scanned the horizon.

Price followed her through the main door - closing and locking it behind them - whilst Mary walked in to the kitchen.

She initially ignored him - not that she was being rude or dismissive. Instead, she was filling the kettle with water, to make them both some tea.

Price's phone buzzed again, just as Mary turned to face him.

BUMMER: I CAN'T FIND HER. WATCH OUT

Mary smiled as she walked forward and looked down at Price's phone, instantly reading the message upside down.

Neither had spoken at this point. However, she broke the silence - reaching out to take the device, "May I?"

Price handed her the phone so that she could reply.

PRICE: THIS IS MARY. HE'S FINE HE'S WITH ME :)
PRICE: THERE'S A HOTEL UP THE ROAD
PRICE: SEE YOU IN THE MORNING
BUMMER: WHAT?

Whilst laughing, Price took his phone back and replied again.

PRICE: SHE'S FINE AND SO AM I SHREW
PRICE: FEEL FREE TO COME HERE OR THE HOTEL
PRICE: YOUR CHOICE MATE

Bummer read the reply in amazement, mixed with an element of amusement.

He knew that Price was the only person to call him Shrew. That would have been deliberate to confirm his identity. So, he walked further up the road towards the small hotel Mary had referred to, and checked in.

Price looked at Mary and, with a determined more assertive voice, said, "I can assure you, I have not been followed. Not this time."

"I wouldn't be so sure darling. I suspect this is not what you think it is. But anyway, enough of that for tonight. You owe me sex."

Price sighed, "If you're right, how long have we got?"

"I don't know."

"We need to talk. I want to know."

"Not tonight," Mary interrupted with a louder, harsh tone in her voice. Then, instantly switching to a softer tone, she added, "Not tonight darling. We probably have one night before we're found. So, let's just enjoy a few hours of pleasure together. We can speak in the morning."

Price looked at Mary's expression - desperately trying to read her mind.

This wasn't the calm, unshakeably cool lady he knew and loved. She almost had a sense of panic. Her words sounded like this could be the last time - their final chance to be together.

For a few moments, he just stared at her - wondering what had happened. What had she done or what had happened that meant she was in so much trouble.

"It can wait," he told himself. "I guess it will have to."

So, instead of challenging her, he said, "I'd hate to be disturbed at an inconvenient moment. We need to set up some basic alarms so we're not caught out."

Mary smiled as she led Price upstairs to the bedroom.

"How do you think I found you? I have a perimeter of infrared alarms. It's how I spotted you and your friend. If anything, or anyone, larger than a rabbit comes within a hundred yards, we'll know. Relax."

"Why did you go to the café?"

Mary laughed, "To check out your friend of course. I wanted to see whose side he was on. You know how I operate, so I'm sure you already knew that darling."

Price acknowledged the remark - adding, "He's on our side."

"Yes, I worked that out. Although, he looks more like a soldier than a spy darling."

"He is a soldier. A damned good soldier at that."

Mary just smiled back as she grabbed Price's hand and pulled him towards the bed - very gently touching his lips with her finger whilst whispering, "No more work for tonight."

Despite that, Price couldn't help checking his mobile phone one more time - immediately seeing a new encrypted message from the Chief of Staff.

SIS: WE FINALLY MANAGED TO ID THE BIKERS

SIS: THE ONES YOU SHOT IN LONDON
SIS: THE CLUE WAS THAT CLASSICAL MUSIC. THE WALTZ
SIS: THERE WAS A PSYCHO CASE ABOUT IT
SIS: THE SUBJECT OF THE CASE WAS SLAVIC STEPKA
SIS: THE BIKERS WERE THE NERVE AGENT COURIER
SIS: AND ONE WAS SLAVIC STEPKA'S BROTHER!!
SIS: STEPKA WILL KNOW HE'S DEAD
SIS: WE DON'T KNOW IF HE KNOWS YOU KILLED HIM
SIS: BE CAREFUL!!!!

Price read the message in amazement - stunned that all the events over the past weeks and months, were potentially linked in some way.

"First there was Vitaly Isaev and the deadly nerve agent attack. Then the brutal murders in the restaurant and hotel, then the bikers and Mary. And now Slavic Stepka. Where does Alexei fit in to all this mess?" he wondered.

He sent a simple reply:

PRICE: SO HE'S HERE FOR REVENGE?
SIS: NOT CONFIRMED
SIS: BUT IF HE KNOWS YOU KILLED HIS BROTHER...
PRICE: UNDERSTOOD. HE'LL BE AFTER ME
PRICE: HAVE MADE CONTACT WITH MARY
PRICE: WILL INTERROGATE HER
SIS: SHE IS EXPENDIBLE. DON'T FORGET THAT!!

Reading the last message from the Chief of Staff, Price couldn't help smiling, whilst also thinking, "You are a cold heartless bastard sometimes." So, he replied:

PRICE: AREN'T WE ALL

Price hadn't realised that Mary was looking over his shoulder, until she whispered, "You're supposed to be in bed."

Price looked back at her and just nodded - shutting off his phone in the process.

"He's right you know," she added, whilst leaning over to kiss him.

"I know. So was I with my reply."

"I know darling. That's why we are here."

"Waiting?"

"Yes darling. We are waiting. This way the killer comes to us. Then only two people are at risk and not dozens of innocent families. There have been far too many deaths. We have to stop the killer and bring this to an end."

Price nodded his agreement.

He knew that Mary was right. But as was typical of his personality, he couldn't resist making light of their situation - if only to remove some of the tension from the air.

"So, us here in this room. Waiting. In some respects, it's a bit like the last scene in Butch Cassidy and the Sundance Kid, don't you think? You know? When they've escaped to Bolivia and they're in that small room about to burst out and try and make their escape."

Mary started laughing as she punched Price in the arm and said, "What are you on about? It's nothing like that. And anyway, they died if you remember?"

"Ah, but did they? They never showed that in the film. I mean, we are all supposed to assume they died. But that's just an assumption. It's all part of the legend that makes it such a good movie."

"They died Price. Everyone knows that - except for you it seems. Get over it."

"I'm not sure they did die."

"Really? What the fuck is wrong with you darling? You cannot be serious."

"What I meant was."

Price was about to continue, when Mary grabbed a pillow and covered his mouth.

"They died. Now shut the fuck up. Let's enjoy the night."

Then, removing the pillow, her hand gently snaked its way down between his legs.

As Price felt her hand grab at his groin, his eyes lit up and he said, "Oh, well if you put it like that."

11. Waiting

It was still dark when the alarm sounded on Mary's phone.

Price was already wide awake, even though his eyes were still closed. He had been listening to the birds in the trees outside - their morning calls, just as the sun rose above the horizon.

Something in his subconscious had told him that an alert was imminent. He couldn't explain why - he just had a feeling.

"Maybe it's because it's what I would have done," he thought.

On hearing the quiet beeping, Price leapt out of the bed - somewhat surprised to see Mary was already dressed and standing by the door.

"Sorry, I couldn't sleep darling," she explained as Price got dressed.

"I couldn't really sleep either. I was waiting for the alarm. I had a bad feeling we would have a visitor."

Mary acknowledged Price with a half-smile, as he said, "How far away are the alarms anyway? You said something about a hundred yards, right?"

Mary nodded, "A little less than that actually," as she picked up her monocular and switched on the infrared light in a single swift movement.

"We should have a few minutes. Unless he's moving really fast. Let's get down stairs. The stone wall out the front provides an excellent firing position."

Price didn't need to be asked twice - quickly checking his gun was loaded and ready to be fired.

It was too late though.

Before they could even open the bedroom door, two loud shotgun blasts were followed by an almighty thud, as the front door crashed to the floor, signalling that they were no longer alone.

Mary gave Price a rather worried glance as she said, "So much for the wall. Let's get out the back via that window. There's a terrace and another good position for us to take him out, down by the river."

Price walked over to the window. Then, standing to the side of the frame, he grabbed the curtain, pulling it back to let some natural light in to the room - quickly scanning the outside.

The wooden-decked terrace at the back of the cottage appeared, at first glance, to be empty.

Looking back in to the room, he hesitated, then asked, "Who is it? Is it Alexei? Or is it Slavic Stepka?"

"I very much doubt that it's Alexei darling. He's far subtler than this. I suspect this is Slavic Stepka. I didn't realise you knew him?"

"I don't really know him. At least, not socially."

"He's not your type Price."

Price nodded, "Yeah, I heard."

"He works for me. Or rather, he used to work for me."

"And now he wants you dead?"

Mary smiled, "Yes. One of many people who would quite like to see me dead, darling."

Price stared directly in to Mary's eyes. He wanted to know the truth as he asked, "Was he the man in the restaurant and the hotel?"

Mary didn't try and hide her answer. She just gave an emotionless, "Yes."

"And Alexei?"

"He needs to die. In fact, one way or another, he must die!"

Price had many more questions, but time was short. The stone floor of the old cottage amplified the intruder's footsteps.

Not only were they getting louder by the second, they were interspersed with shotgun blasts at every corner of the building.

Price gave a small nod towards the window - eliciting immediate agreement from Mary.

As they quietly climbed out on to the wooden terrace at the rear of the cottage, the bedroom door rattled as the intruder tried the handle.

Faced with a locked door, they both knew what would be next and turned to climb down to the river bank.

What they didn't realise, however, was that a second intruder lay in wait.

Just as they turned, a calm voice with a strong Russian accent stopped them dead in their tracks.

"Don't move or I will have to shoot. Drop your guns."

Price and Mary froze, then slowly reached down and let their pistols drop on to the wooden decking before turning to their right - both, immediately recognising the man behind the voice.

"Price, this is an unexpected pleasure."

"Likewise, Alexei. It's good to see you too. However, I'm afraid we don't have much time for pleasantries."

Price was about to explain that Slavic Stepka was probably about to burst in to the bedroom, when two more loud bangs signalled the end of the door.

Alexei glanced to the bedroom window with his gun still pointing at Price and Mary.

Price later recalled that the events which followed, happened so fast, it was difficult to tell exactly which order they occurred in.

He was sure he saw Mary move out of the corner of his eye. He certainly heard her shout, "Wait!"

He also heard Alexei shout, "Stop, it's me." which he initially had thought was directed at Mary - only later realising that it was aimed at Slavic Stepka.

Not that either of their actions had any effect - unlike the two loud cracks and flashes from the bedroom window. They had devastating effects.

The first shot ripped Alexei's abdomen apart - turning it in to a gruesome mixture of blood and shredded intestines, as he collapsed to the floor - his internal organs spilling out on to the deck in the process.

The second shot sent Mary hurtling backwards over the side of the terrace - a drop of six feet down on to the edge of the grass river bank below.

Price went to move, but a third blast to the wooden decking by his feet, stopped him.

Slavic Stepka climbed through the window as if it were nothing more than a small step. Then the huge man walked forward - with a slight limp, Price observed.

The shotgun was raised and pointing at Price's chest.

Price had spent many hours with SIS psycho-analysts. He knew he had many faults and he knew that his mind had been damaged by all the events and horrors he had witnessed over the years.

However, he also knew how to behave when he was confronted by an armed assassin - even one as professional as Slavic Stepka.

Obviously, it wasn't something he looked forward to, and it was certainly to be avoided wherever possible. But it wasn't something he feared. It was something to be managed and controlled.

He'd handled it on a number of occasions before, and was in no doubt that he would do so again.

Looking straight at Slavic Stepka, he deliberately made eye contact as he casually said, "Thank you."

"What for?"

"For not shooting me dead in the hotel. You let me

escape. Thank you. I am much obliged."

Slavic Stepka's face displayed an element of surprise, which told Price he had succeeded. He had touched a nerve in the man's brain and in doing so had created a connection between them - something that, in the immediate short term, would keep him alive and enable him to start a conversation.

And that's the key. The golden rule. Because, whilst they're speaking to you, they're less likely to be firing their weapon at you.

Slavic Stepka paused for a few seconds as he thought about Price's remarks. Then he said, "You're welcome. Call it professional courtesy. We are both just doing our jobs right, Price?"

Price maintained eye contact as he asked, "Are you honestly telling me you're acting under orders? I find that a little difficult to believe."

Before Slavic Stepka could reply, both men heard a groan and looked down at Alexei who, remarkably, was just about still alive.

Sadly, not for long though. Slavic Stepka discharged another shotgun round - this time directly at Alexei's face.

Price quickly looked away.

He wasn't particularly squeamish, but he had no desire to remember the image of Alexei's disintegrated face - that would just add to all the horrors he wished he'd never witnessed.

"These two were my orders," Slavic Stepka replied, as he returned the shotgun to its original position, a few feet in front of Price's chest.

"Hopefully, I'm not on the list as well," Price remarked, somewhat flippantly.

"If you had been, you wouldn't be alive now. But this is your second chance. There will not be a third chance Price."

"Well, thanks again. It seems I am in your debt."

"Climb down there," Slavic Stepka added - pointing to the river bank with the shotgun. "Go and cry over your dead girlfriend. Leave your gun here."

Price nodded and turned to face the river.

All his training told him that he should not turn his back on an armed assailant. His instincts, however, told him otherwise.

This would be fine. Slavic Stepka was a disturbed, sick, murderer who, fortunately, appeared to be unaware that Price was the person who killed his brother. And for some inexplicable reason, seemed to believe in some kind of honour amongst fellow professionals.

"If the tables were turned," Price mused, whilst he climbed down to the river bank, "You'd be well and truly dead by now. There is no honour amongst spies. What there is, is a bloody big fight."

Looking back up, Price could see that Slavic Stepka had taken the opportunity to leave - which made sense. After all, his mission was now complete.

Price didn't care.

He crouched down on the grass river bank next to Mary,

who was not moving.

Strangely, there didn't seem to be the same massive blood loss and devastation that he'd seen on Alexei. But even so, as he leaned forward to check her vital signs, he felt sure this was the end.

Before he could be certain, however, Price heard shouting.

He looked up, only to see Bummer, who was a hundred yards away and sprinting at full speed along the river bank. He was shouting for Price to go after Slavic Stepka.

"Go after him. I'll take care of her. Go! You're nearest. Go and get him! Shoot him in the back!"

Price looked down at Mary than back at Bummer.

His heart wanted to stay, but he knew what he should do. So, with a wave to Bummer he quickly climbed back up to the terrace, retrieved his gun and dived through the open window into the bedroom before immediately jumping to his feet and sprinting through the cottage as fast as his legs would carry him.

Price knew that, if Slavic Stepka had decided to remain in the cottage, then this would make him an easy target. But he was sure in his mind that the assassin would have left.

Most likely, he'd be walking away from the cottage - probably to the nearest road, where he would have left his car. Close enough, but out of sight.

With that in mind, Price ran out of the hole where the front door had been blown apart and crouched down by the stone wall - the same stone wall they had intended to use as a firing position and that Mary had used to evade him the previous day.

Price stopped and listened. The only sound being his own breathing, occasionally interrupted by birdsongs as the woods woke up to the sunlight of the day.

Suddenly, Price's head moved as he heard something else - something that didn't fit.

"Yes," he thought, "That's it," as he closed his eyes to identify the direction of the sound - the sound of feet trampling and crushing leaves and wood on the ground - a clear indication of where Slavic Stepka was.

Price jumped to his feet and ran forward - gun raised - being careful not to make the same mistake and give away his location.

As he sped up from a run to a fully-fledged sprint, Price finally saw Slavic Stepka in the distance. He was covering the ground quite quickly, but clearly wasn't expecting to be followed.

Around two hundred yards ahead of him, Price could see that Slavic Stepka had arrived at his car.

"I may be too late," he thought, as he stopped - feeling his heart racing as he tried to control his breathing.

Slavic Stepka got in via the driver's door just as Price breathed out to steady his aim before firing two shots in quick succession.

Both shots hit the car, just as it started to move. The first passing through the driver's door - the second through the driver's window.

Price could see Slavic Stepka look back in to the woods

and, judging by the way he moved, he was sure that at least one bullet had reached its target.

It didn't, however, stop the car from accelerating violently away - speeding down the road in to the distance as Price fired again and again whilst running forward.

The bullets smashed the car's back window, but even that didn't stop it rounding a bend in the distance, where Price lost sight of his target.

He messaged the Chief of Staff in order to try and trace the vehicle - although he didn't expect any success. He knew that Slavic Stepka was a professional and would change to a new vehicle very quickly - at which point they would have lost him.

With that in mind, Price turned and slowly made his way back to the cottage - an overwhelming sense of tragedy filling his mind.

He was sure that he would find Mary dead next to the river. The one person in the world he cared about more than anyone else.

Part of him almost didn't want to look - the feelings of dread almost making him feel sick in his stomach, as he walked around the side of the cottage to the grass bank by the river.

To his horror, he found Bummer laying on the ground barely conscious, and Mary gone.

It turned out that Bummer had leaned down to check Mary's breathing, just as she regained consciousness.

In her disorientated and wounded state, she hadn't immediately recognised Bummer. So, with all her remaining strength, she had lashed out with her right leg, landing a violent blow to the underside of Bummer's jaw.

Bummer had been propelled backwards - clutching his face in agony - whilst Mary, in an attempt to escape, had rolled her body to the side.

Unfortunately, it had been a roll to her right - placing herself in the fast current of the river, that carried her away.

The many hours of searching that followed, proved fruitless.

Given the shotgun blast, the fall and the fast current of the icy cold river, when the police divers and search teams finally gave up, the Chinese Embassy was contacted.

Mary was listed as missing, presumed dead. Or, as a coroner later recorded it, death by misadventure.

12. Enemy By Association

Weeks passed, as depression consumed Price's very being.

Even in his brief moments of level-headedness, he couldn't think of anything or anyone else, such was the all-consuming nature of his grief.

The thought that his friend and lover was gone, left him in a state of shock.

Price had seen many people die over the years. Some by his side and some by his own hands. But he had never before lost someone quite so dear to him. Someone who had touched his heart.

Sitting at his desk in SIS's headquarters, he just stared blankly at the computer screen. His mind numbed to the surroundings - his eyes frozen in a trance-like state.

The Chief had seen the symptoms before - having lost agents on operations and observed the effect on their friends and colleagues.

He knew it was never easy to come to terms with a huge loss. Even he sometimes struggled to relegate events to the back of his mind - knowing that, as the Firm's leader, he regularly had to make life and death decisions. Whilst also knowing that, if they went wrong, he would have to live with the consequences of those decisions for the rest of his life.

On seeing Price's depression, he arranged meetings with

the in-house counsellor who very quick advised a vacation, in order to take time to come to terms with the loss.

However, Price politely declined. He wanted to keep himself busy and thought he could do that by reading the latest European intelligence reports - something that he typically tried to avoid at all costs.

By his own admission, Price was a blunt instrument.

He wasn't someone you could hand millions of lines of data with the expectation of receiving back a comprehensive analysis with projections that would lead to an arrest or the prevention of a terrorist attack.

"I'm more your point and squirt person," he was often quoted as saying. "Point me in the right direction, and I'll squirt the target with a ton of lead or perhaps some C4 explosive, if I feel so inclined."

However, losing Mary started to make him re-think his approach. Maybe he'd seen too many deaths. Maybe this was the last time he ever wanted to be involved.

Maybe it was time to do something else.

Privately, the SIS Chief was far less philosophical.

Now that they had positively identified the attacker as Slavic Stepka, he intended to take action.

In a secret meeting behind closed doors with nobody else listening, he said to the Chief of Staff, "I want him removed and I don't care how. Although, it's probably better if nobody knows it was us because I don't have approval. Not yet, anyway. We're still discussing it at the highest levels of government."

The Chief of Staff nodded his agreement and then asked, "D'you think it would be something Price could do? Maybe give him a sense of closure?"

"No. He's far too emotionally involved. In his current mental state, he's liable to behave irrationally and make matters worse. Find someone else. Someone who doesn't care. Someone who's just doing their job.

In fact, get someone to push Stepka in front of a train at a station so that it appears to be an accident.

Price needs to have time to consign this to history and pull himself together again - as I've no doubt he will. But we need to give him time to do that."

The Chief of Staff completely agreed with the Chief's assessment. He knew that, in truth, he'd only asked because of his loyalty and respect for Price as a friend.

Price had said, "Tell me when you find him. Please. Let me deal with him."

That said, even Price, in his heart, knew that he was too emotionally involved. He just didn't care. This was personal and, in his mind, the impact was so great that it made the usual rules an annoying irrelevance.

On hearing the Chief's decision, he immersed himself even more deeply in the intelligence reports.

"If they won't tell me where he is, then I'll find him myself," he thought. "They can't stop me taking a holiday and accidentally pushing the bastard off a cliff or perhaps in front of a submachine gun that just happens to be firing on automatic at the time."

The problem was, Slavic Stepka had vanished.

There were no reported sightings by anyone in SIS, by their agents abroad or even by partner agencies around the world. And make no mistake, SIS has been around a very long time. They know everyone who's worth knowing.

"It's crazy," Price related to Chas. "I can't understand it. He's vanished off the face of the earth. That doesn't happen these days. Everyone leaves a trail in the modern world - whether it's credit cards, going to the ATM, a mobile phone or facial recognition from CCTV cameras. It's not possible to vanish unless you just hide in a hole and never go out!"

Chas agreed but tried to calm Price down.

"Yeah, it's messed up mate. But I can't help thinking, maybe it's for the best. I dislike him as much as you. I think you know that. Until he shows up, let's just put him out of our minds and move on mate."

Whilst Price appreciated the sentiment, he continued searching undeterred - unaware, at least initially, that he wasn't the only one doing so.

The other searcher was a thousand miles away in the capital of Slovakia - taking a very different approach.

With young twins - who in this case were two little girls - a parent's job can be very tiring whilst at the same time, extremely rewarding.

On this evening, just after dusk, a family of four were getting ready to go out. They were planning to visit some friends a couple of miles away on the far side of Slovakia's capital city, Bratislava.

The twins were dressed in matching floral-patterned outfits, befitting their young age. The cutest of looks that would make any parent across the world smile. And, rather unusually for toddlers their age, they were waiting patiently - sitting in their high-chairs at the family dining room table whilst their mother scurried around, making last minute preparations.

Like all good mothers, she had what can only be described as, her bag of stuff.

It was a large sports bag that contained the essential items you need to care for a couple of toddlers. A change of clothes, spare underwear, soft drinks, a towel, the obligatory wet wipes - arguably one of the greatest inventions the world has ever created where young children are concerned - and of course, some of their favourite toys.

In this case, the toys were a small, rather tired, brown teddy bear and a plastic doll of a female superhero.

As the mother placed the doll in the bag, she and her husband exchanged looks - reading each other's mind as only a husband and wife can.

They were remembering a private joke where, only a few days earlier, they had observed that the doll looked more like some kind of leather-clad sexual dominatrix than a superhero. Something they would enjoy laughing over with their daughters - albeit in at least another fifteen or so years, when it would become part of the family's history.

The husband - the toddlers' father - put his shoes on and

looked back at his family from the front door.

To his left, the children had started giggling as they watched their mum struggling with the zip on the bag.

It was too full and, consequently, kept resisting her attempts to close it. As a result, she was becoming increasingly aggravated - quietly cursing at it under her breath.

Walking forwards to help, her husband only managed to take two steps before it happened.

The figure - completely dressed in black and wearing a tinted motorbike helmet to obscure all facial features - had placed explosives around frame of the back door to the house, which erupted.

The initial blinding flash of light was accompanied, almost instantaneously, by a deafening bang.

Microseconds later, fragments of masonry, wood and glass were propelled in all directions - fortunately not quite reaching the twins seated at the table.

However, what had moments before been a typical happy family scene, was in an instant replaced by a dust filled room.

The children were screaming at the top of their lungs, as their parents ran forward and threw their arms around them.

Then, as the dust cloud gradually started to settle, the family were able to see the effects of the explosion.

Where they used to have a back door to their house, was now a large gaping hole. A hole where the black-clad figure stood, armed with a Heckler & Koch MP5SD3 submachine gun.

For a second, seeing the dark figure, the family froze. Nobody spoke. Even the children were briefly silenced by fear - to the point where, the only sound was some cracking and creaking as the rear wall of the house struggled to maintain its integrity after such a violent blast.

Then the firing started.

The suppressed thuds of the silenced bullets struck walls, furniture, the ceiling and the floor - shredding anything and everything in their path.

The family - amazingly - survived the initial onslaught and, fearing for their lives, fled in to the street at the front of the house - the mother and father running in to the historical cobbled lane outside their home, each carrying a screaming and terrified twin.

As they ran for their lives, the attacker followed them through the front door and continued the brutal onslaught.

Cars parked to their left and right burst in to flames. Overhead lighting and street signs were shattered. The attacker - apparently unconcerned about the lives of bystanders - was firing, not only down the street, but at the surrounding buildings as well - evidently determined to create complete and utter mayhem.

It was only as the family reached the end of the road and were about to turn a corner, that the firing finally stopped.

The mother glanced back - seeing the burning cars and

the shop windows smashed to pieces - the horror of the scene combined with relief that they were alive, filling her mind.

Then, just as she was about to look away, an almighty explosion sent shivers down her spine.

Their house and home crumbled before her eyes - the shockwave sending bricks and mortar flying in to the street, whilst a smoke plume rose above - seconds later becoming engulfed in fire, when the falling masonry severed a gas main buried in the road.

The figure in black, however, was gone - nowhere to be seen.

The family spent two weeks with police protection.

They were staying in a small, local hotel where their room was guarded twenty-four hours a day - whilst the mother and father were asked endless questions about their potential enemies.

They tried to cooperate, but there were no obvious suspects.

As the father declared, "We're just a family. We don't have enemies. I work at the train station and my wife works at a nursery. We do our jobs and go home and bring up our children."

But it wasn't to be that simple.

On a quiet Sunday afternoon with very few people around, the family left the hotel.

They only had to walk a few meters from the front door of the hotel building and out in to the road where the police cars were waiting.

As a purely precautionary measure, the road had been closed to traffic and police officers had formed a line between the door and the car - just in case there was another attack. Although, nobody really expected there to be any trouble.

The police inspector in charge was even heard to comment, "This is a ridiculous use of my officers who would be far more productive deployed elsewhere."

However, as the family emerged, four shots were fired in quick succession. So quickly that, later the same day when interviewed, most witnesses were unable to accurately describe how many shots had been fired.

The general consensus was that there had been a loud bang like a car back-firing. Although, some of the more knowledgeable witnesses observed that the bang lasted longer than they would have expected.

All four family members were shot and fell to the ground before their police guards could even react.

Some of the more junior officers attempted to return fire. A futile attempt that the inspector halted by bellowing his instructions above the gunfire, in order to be heard.

Whilst he had been sceptical about the operation, his experience told him that the attacker was gone.

He was right.

A further two weeks later, the police allowed the family to make a second attempt at leaving - this time from the hospital.

It turned out that all four bullets had only been glancing blows. They had torn away skin but caused no lasting damage. The stay in hospital had been to allow the police to conduct further investigations, rather than for medical reasons.

When they did leave, however, the security was far more comprehensive, if not positively extreme.

They left via a rarely-used exit that was surrounded on three sides by the hospital building itself - with a police officer being stationed at every window overlooking the small courtyard.

Their route from the hospital door to the unmarked police Range Rover was protected by a forth wall. A wall of heavily armed officers wearing body armour, who were assigned to take them to a secure location.

The father was first, at his insistence - closely followed by his wife and then two officers who carried the children - each wrapped in a bullet proof blanket.

Once they were inside the armoured Range Rover and the doors were locked, the children moved to sit between their parents - the father on the left - his wife on the right.

Then, with their seat belts secure and the road outside declared clear, a convoy of cars and 4x4's made their way out of the courtyard - police bikes riding either side of the Range Rover - more armoured vehicles travelling in front and behind.

A convoy of this kind might seem like a good idea - and indeed, it does provide protection for a vehicle when there are other cars before and after. However, unless the drivers of all the vehicles are extremely well-trained and have rehearsed manoeuvres to respond to incidents, it also traps the vehicle.

It limits their escape options if they are attacked, because they are also blocked-in. It makes it more difficult for them to act spontaneously, which is why pre-agreed responses are key.

Something the police had, sadly, not realised would be necessary.

The onslaught as the Range Rover made its way down the public road, was something that one officer later likened to a war zone.

Nobody in the force had experienced or seen anything like it before - the ferocity and the number of bullets.

It began as the armoured Range Rover reached what you might call, the point of no return.

They were a hundred yards from the protection of the hospital courtyard, surrounded by the other vehicles and, therefore, unable to easily turn back.

The police later estimated that over a thousand rounds had been fired.

Whilst the windows of the Range Rover were bullet proof, such was the intensity of the attack, even they eventually shattered - bringing the vehicle to a halt as the driver took cover, fearing for his life.

Cowering down, shielded only by the armour-plated bodywork, the family and their police guards could feel the rounds striking the vehicle as it rocked from side to side from the force of the impacts - collapsing on to the wheel rims as the reinforced tyres were torn to shreds.

Then came the eerie silence as the firing stopped.

A policeman, who had thrown himself on top of the children to prevent them from sitting up, started to move, whilst telling the family to stay down below the level of the windows - fearing that the attacker was reloading.

He was wrong though. There were no more bullets.

Instead, there was something far worse.

The rocket-propelled grenade struck the underside of the engine compartment - having been fired with pin-point accuracy.

In a fraction of a second, it ripped the front of the vehicle apart.

From the inside, all the family knew was, there was an almighty bang as the front of the Range Rover lifted off the ground. Then, less than a second later, it crashed back down and collapsed - the body being ripped apart in the process.

The children screamed in terror as police officers from surrounding vehicles, not caring for their own lives, ran to their rescue.

Then, unfortunately, they made their mistake.

Fearing further grenade attacks, the police tried to get the family out of the vehicle.

Surrounded by a huddle of armed officers, the father took a single step outside.

His wife and children would have followed, but were not given the opportunity.

The bullet that struck the father's leg, found its target via a three-inch gap between police arms, legs and body armour. And this time, it was not a glancing blow.

It cracked a bone, causing him to fall to the ground in agony, as the police officers hurriedly surrounded the Range Rover with more of their own cars, to prevent further shots from being possible.

Then slowly, but carefully, they towed the family in what remained of the Range Rover, back in to the hospital courtyard and to relative safety.

Back in London, Price read the news reports as well as the initial police report, before turning to the detailed assessment from both his own service and the local Slovakian intelligence service.

It was the skill and precision of the attacks that caught his attention.

These weren't the actions of a bitter and twisted betrayed husband or wife out for revenge. This wasn't even a thief trying to escape from a crime scene.

This was a highly skilled professional who for some reason was playing with their prey. It was someone with the same level of skills as Slavic Stepka.

"Why would anyone want to hurt that family," he wondered, just as the Chief of Staff walked in to his office.

"Busy?"

Price looked up and nodded no.

The Chief of Staff nodded to the office door as he said, "Let's go. Meeting room 111."

Price didn't reply. He just stood up, emptied his pockets and followed the Chief of Staff out of his office - locking the door behind him.

Price had been to that meeting room before. It was the most secure meeting room in the SIS building that was traditionally named after the organisation's age.

Whilst the entire SIS building is shielded from all forms of electromagnetic radiation to prevent eavesdropping from the outside, room 111 has its own additional protection measures - plus, all those who enter are thoroughly scanned and searched.

No documents ever refer to the room and nobody officially acknowledges that it even exists. The unwritten but strictly followed rule is that, nothing said in the meeting room can ever be repeated outside, under any circumstances.

As they passed through security, Price remembered a number of so-called black-ops he'd been assigned to from the room. Meetings that inevitably ended with the Chief saying, "You're on your own. Good luck."

Price and the Chief of Staff sat down opposite the SIS Chief, who spoke first.

"D'you see the papers describing those attacks on a family in Bratislava. A professional by all accounts?"

Price nodded agreement and said, "Yeah. I know it's not really appropriate, but you have to respect the skill of the shooter. Obviously, he's cruel and presumably deranged in some way, but rather talented nevertheless.

Why though? They're just a normal family. They're people

doing their stuff. Going about their lives."

The Chief smiled - a smile that clearly indicated he knew something Price didn't.

"Go on," Price asked. "What is it? What do you know that I don't Sir?"

"The woman Price. She's married."

"And?"

"Do you know what her maiden name was?"

A suspicious expression answered the question for Price, but he spoke anyway, "No, but I'm suspecting you're about to tell me."

"Stepka."

Price smiled, "Oh wow! That changes it somewhat."

"It does don't you think?"

"She's his sister, right? A dumb question I know, but stranger things have happened in this ever-so messed up world."

The Chief nodded. "It's her. Slovakian immigration shared her passport details, birth certificate and parents' marriage certificate. We cross-referenced that with a copy of Slavic Stepka's birth certificate that they also provided. It all checks out. And if she's in trouble, you know what that means."

"He'll surely go and help her."

"I would."

"As I would I. But who's the shooter Sir?"

The Chief shrugged his shoulders. "We don't know. Could be the Chinese after revenge for the killing of Mary. Or maybe the Russians trying to flush out Stepka in order to silence a rogue agent. In any case Price, in the light of this new information, I'm assigning the task to you. But, this is not official, which is why we are here, in this room."

The Chief looked around the room - the almost mundane surroundings, given the importance of the room. Then, making eye contact with Price, he said, "You cannot step out of line on this one. I expect this to be executed as a cold-hearted task. It needs to be as if you had never met and he was a complete stranger to you. Is that clear?"

Price nodded. "I understand Sir. This is not personal. It's a task and nothing more. But, if you don't mind me asking. What made you change your mind? About me, that is?"

The Chief smiled, "It's been a few weeks and everyone tells me that you're coping well and coming to terms with what happened. I see it as well. You're clearly over the initial shock and heartache.

You and I go back a long way. So, I'm giving you a chance to put it behind you. I'm trusting you Price and I'm taking a leap of faith."

Price nodded, "Much appreciated Sir. Be assured, I won't let you down."

"As if you didn't already know, your task is to find and eliminate Slavic Stepka - most likely, when he arrives in Bratislava."

Price hesitated then said, "It would be good if we can try and get some more intel on the shooter."

At that point, the Chief of Staff interrupted, "Agreed.

Sadly, there's nothing to go on at the moment. Funnily enough, you're the only good suspect, as you have a motive and the skills."

Price laughed, "Fair point Sir. I certainly do have the motive and on a good day, the ability. I'd follow me if I were you."

The Chief of Staff gave a knowing smile, as he said, "We regularly do follow you, as you know very well."

Price laughed again before adding, "You might think I'd be offended Sir. But actually, that makes sense."

The Chief of Staff ignored Price and continued speaking.

"There's only one decent photo where our shooter walked in to the street after the first attack. Sadly, even that's quite poor quality as it was from a traffic camera."

Price looked at a photo before asking, "I presume we've done the analysis. Estimated height and weight, etc."

"Yes. He's not a big Russian assassin like your friend Alexei was. Or Slavic Stepka. This one is considerably smaller. It's difficult to make a precise measurement as he appears to be wearing a lot of body armour and head gear."

"So, we've really no idea?" Price asked.

"He's not very tall and probably quite slim under all that gear. Maybe one-sixty to one-seventy in height. We're trying to find a match based on that, but it's like a needle in a haystack. There are thousands out there. You know how it is. We use people of all shapes and sizes ourselves, for that precise reason."

"Well, whoever he is, he's good."

The Chief of Staff nodded, "You're not wrong there. D'you want to hear the best part?"

"What?"

The Chief of Staff leaned over and typed on the conference room computer keyboard to bring up the traffic cam video of the original attack on the family.

"Watch this, it's a video that we only just received from Slovakian intelligence," he said, as they saw the black figure emerge from the house, followed by the destructive effects of the gunfire.

When the video started, the street had been fairly busy, with people walking along, going about their business. However, by the end, it was just as if an army had declared war - smashed cars and shops, some of which were on fire - water spurting from fire hydrants, glass and building materials strewn across the road.

"How many shots do you think were fired?"

Price thought back to the police report he'd read minutes before, as he said, "It was in the hundreds, maybe even a thousand, wasn't it?"

"Local cops now reckon it was well over a thousand - same as the latest attack."

"That's insane."

"Guess how many people died or were injured?"

"I dread to think Sir. Too many."

"None."

"What?"

"None. Except for a few cuts and bruises and people falling over whilst running away, which doesn't really count does it."

"And the second attack was just flesh wounds, right?" Price added.

"Yep, flesh wounds to the family's legs. Just grazes. They were more like scratches than gunshot wounds."

"That's what I mean about skill Sir. That's not an easy shot to take on a moving target, let alone four moving targets in quick succession."

"I know," the Chief of Staff agreed.

"The father got hit in the third attack, right?"

"The father of the family took a bullet to his leg, yes. Non-fatal. It hit a bone, which will be repaired with no permanent damage. Our shooter was very careful to avoid any key muscles or an artery."

Price laughed, "That's crazy isn't it Sir. A professional assassin discharged, over three separate incidents, in excess of a couple of thousand rounds, and not a single person was killed?"

"No. It's far more remarkable than that," the Chief of Staff replied. "It wasn't just two thousand rounds. There was a rocket-propelled grenade on the last attack if you recall. And, not only was nobody killed, nobody apart from a few silly incidents and one broken leg, was even injured."

Price nodded, "Yeah this shooter is seriously talented as I say. Because during the first attack it was a crowded street, and the shooting was all over the place."

"It was Price, you're right. The thousands of rounds went in all directions. Cars caught fire, buildings caught fire. But not randomly. Our analysts have worked through the CCTV footage frame by frame. That shooter missed every single pedestrian. And when cars were lit up, they were only the ones that had nobody inside or standing next to them at the time. As you've said, there's no doubt about the fact that this was skilfully executed. Deliberately so."

"Because."

"The shooter wanted to send a message."

Price nodded, "The shooter wants Slavic Stepka and not his family or some innocent passer-by."

"Precisely."

Price looked at the Chief of Staff before glancing back at the only photo they had of the person dressed in black - the initial cam shot showing the rear view.

"So, dumb question. What happens if I come face to face with the shooter? Do I take him out as well?"

"Avoid it at all costs, if you can. The shooter is not our problem. Let the local forces deal with him."

"The shooter is bound to see me."

"Well let's hope for your sake it turns out to be someone who's not too trigger happy."

Price smiled, as he wasn't concerned.

"This shooter is a true pro Sir. We should be OK. He's clearly not after me, and provided I don't represent a threat - which I'll make sure I don't - I believe he'll do the same. I'd bet money on it."

"And quite possibly your life Price," the Chief added, initially as a joke in rather poor taste - subsequently concluding that, in some respects, it was probably an all too accurate observation.

13. Setting The Trap

Slavic Stepka watched the news with a mixture of horror and despair - thinking, "They killed my brother and now they are trying to kill my sister."

He wanted to scream. He wanted to throw something. He didn't want to hurt anyone in particular, except perhaps the people who were threatening his family.

Mostly though, he just wanted to vent his anger at the world at large. Even though he knew he couldn't, as that would just draw attention to his plight.

Instead, he just sat quietly in the corner of the public bar. A quiet and somewhat gloomy establishment in one of the more rundown parts of east London.

Since fleeing the scene, after shooting Alexei and Mary, Slavic Stepka had been living rough - sleeping in parks and woodlands - using public lavatories to wash.

He had tried to message his masters back in Russia, hoping that, now he had completed his task, they would accept him back so that he could go home. However, despite repeated attempts to contact them, he had received no reply.

He knew that could only be bad news and hated them for it. They had provided him with Mary and Price's location after he escaped from Russia. Then, as soon as the task had been completed, they ignored him.

He knew why. They were waiting. Waiting for him to get

desperate and show his face after which, he too, would be just a piece of history.

"And now this," he thought - finishing his drink and walking out of the bar, pushing past a local man in the process.

The local man had been texting on his mobile phone, and looked up when Slavic Stepka pushed past. His immediate reaction had been to react and challenge the stranger's behaviour.

Fortunately, however, he did a double-take, and on seeing the immense stature of Slavic Stepka walking away, he thought, "Blimey. Yeah, he can push me all he likes. That's fine. I'll even help him if he wants."

For his part, Slavic Stepka barely even noticed the incident. He had decided to take action. He wanted revenge and was heading for a phone box to call in a favour.

Dialling a phone number he had memorised from years before, he waited for the female voice to answer.

"Hello?"

"Hello, it's me. This is an open line."

There was a pause, then the lady said, "I do not know you. Please leave me alone and please do not call this number again."

Slavic Stepka nodded his head from side to side, whilst thinking, "You will not get away that easily."

He said, "Grandma, you know exactly who this is. Let me be very clear so we understand each other. You will help me because I know where you live."

The lady's voice had initially been very professional. However, on hearing the threat, she reverted to her natural east London accent - the tone providing clear evidence of her working-class background.

"Don't you use my name. We can't talk. You're history. Your name's on the list. I 'ave to report any contact with you. You can't phone me. D'you understand?"

Then, with panic setting in, she added, "Get away before you're traced. They'll be after you, you know."

"I need a passport and matching credit card."

"No fuckin' way! We can't do this. You'll get me killed."

"Meet me by the steps in Wapping. Thirty minutes. You know where. I'll give you a passport photo."

There was no reply, so Slavic Stepka hung up the call. He knew she would be there. She had no choice, as he did know where she lived.

Sure enough, thirty minutes later - after using a photo booth at a train station - Slavic Stepka watched his contact walk out of Wapping underground station and turn down Wapping High Street.

Wapping High Street is not a high street in the traditional sense. In years gone by it would have been a bustling thoroughfare, lined with warehouses that backed on to London's River Thames, where ships transported goods to and from the capital.

Now, however, the warehouses have been converted in to expensive apartment blocks, with only the steps remaining as evidence of the area's history - having originally been used to access boats regardless of the water level in the river.

The lady jumped back in surprise, on seeing Slavic Stepka step out of the shadows in front of her. His dark clothing and careful choice of location had made him virtually invisible until the last second.

For his part, he'd forgotten just how petite she was. Standing opposite her, her face barely reached the height of his chest.

Despite it being early evening in a poorly lit corner of London, he could still make out her expression and body language.

She looked cold and scared - wrapped in a thick brown coat with her dark hair covered by a tired-looking grey scarf.

"Were you followed?" he asked.

Looking up at Slavic Stepka's towering figure, she said, "Don't be stupid. Jus' give me the photo."

Slavic Stepka reached in to his pocket and handed over a passport sized photo of himself. Then, looking down at her, he said, "Are you OK?"

She looked at the photo then back up at him.

"What kind of fuckin' question is that? Yeah, I'm fine thanks. Except for some nutter who's trying to get me killed."

Then she paused, before saying, "Look, I'm sorry. I'm fine. Better than you I reckon. You need a wash."

"I'm living on the streets."

"What happened to your arm?"

"It was a bullet wound. It heeled up, but the bullet was still in there and kept hurting. So, last night I dug it out myself. It'll get better."

"You're bleeding. You must stop the bleeding."

"I'll be fine. Anyway, why do you care?"

Ignoring his question, she replied, "This will cost a lot you know."

"I don't have any money."

"Fuck!"

"I want the passport and card tomorrow."

The lady sighed, then said, "OK. But you can't travel looking like that. You look like shit and there's blood everywhere. You'll get stopped and picked up."

"I don't have a choice."

"There's a shelter for the homeless in Whitechapel where you can get cleaned up and have a wash. Go there and for fuck sake shave. And stop that bleeding. I'll bring the stuff to you tomorrow."

Then she wrote the address on a piece of paper and handed it to him.

"If this is a trap."

The lady looked up at him and, whilst making eye contact, shook her head in disbelief.

"If this is a trap, we're both fucked. I'll see you there tomorrow lunchtime. Jus' make sure you're there and don't be late, 'cos I'm not hanging around."

"OK."

The lady put her hands back in her pockets and scurried away whilst, for his part, Slavic Stepka just watched the street. He was still wondering if she had been followed or had reported the meeting to his superiors.

As he looked back and forth, it seemed to be quiet, although he knew he couldn't stay for long. There was every chance that her phone was being monitored.

If so, any number of security services could be arriving imminently. So, with that in mind, he walked away from steps and vanished in to the evening shadows.

As it turned out, Slavic Stepka needn't have been so concerned - his phone call had not triggered an alert.

However, when his face appeared on the CCTV of a London station, entering and leaving a photo booth, that most certainly did. And shortly after, it was GCHQ that raised the alarm.

As the Chief of Staff said to Price later the same evening, "Stepka has got himself a passport photo."

Price sighed, "He'll be going out by car then. We only do visual checks on European passports at that border. And if he's getting a UK passport, they'll probably just let him through with a glance if he picks a busy time."

The Chief of Staff nodded, "Yes, that is a problem. I did float the idea with Border Control that they should check every single passport electronically, but they just laughed."

"Do we know where he's getting the passport from?"

The Chief of Staff smiled. "As you know, there are several people that Five watch for this kind of thing."

"And?"

"They checked the phone records. It's Grandma."

"Really," Price remarked. "That's very interesting. But then, I guess she is the best."

"She's an old friend of yours I believe."

Price nodded, "We've been through quite a lot over the years."

"Ever since you rescued her from that hell hole in Africa, wasn't it?"

Price nodded again, "It was Sir. She used to have an obsession for delivering her product personally and a desire to save the world.

All very honourable, but as she discovered, it can be quite hazardous. She tends to stay put these days and let other people do the dirty work for her."

"Maybe it's time for you to say hello again?"

Price smiled, "Yes Sir, I do believe it is."

"Five are already watching her house. Obviously, if Slavic Stepka turns up, they'll bring him in."

"I very much doubt he'll be that stupid."

"I'm sure you're right. See what you can find out from her

though."

Price nodded agreement and had started to walk away when the Chief of Staff added, very much as an afterthought, "Why is she called Grandma? Isn't she in her thirties?"

Price smiled to himself, as he retrieved his memories of Grandma - stored deep within a very special part of his mind - memories he would never forget.

Then, he turned his head back to face the Chief of Staff and said, "It was in Africa when she helped to save some children, many years ago Sir. The children were terrified and asked her who she was. To calm them down she told them she was their grandma who had come to save them."

"And she did if I recall, didn't she?"

"Pretty much Sir, yes. She's the real deal. A real-life hero in many ways."

The Chief of Staff just shrugged his shoulders. He hadn't really been that interested - it was more idle curiosity than anything else.

As Price drove across London, he remembered how he had first met Grandma.

A lady with a harmless nickname that, at the time, was accompanied by a fearsome reputation - although she'd calmed down a lot since then.

It had been in Nigeria that they first met - not that he knew her at the time.

All he knew was, hundreds of women and children were

being kidnapped by the terrorist group known as Boko Haram.

For those not acquainted with Boko Haram - they are yet another bunch of mentally ill extremists pursuing their own violent perverse jihadist agenda.

To put them in to perspective, they sought to merge with the Islamic State of Iraq and Syria - better known as ISIS - but were rejected for being too extreme.

They're basically rapists, murderers and paedophiles who pretend they believe in a fundamental version of Islam in a futile attempt to validate their repulsive behaviour.

It was a news story about Boko Haram that led to Grandma's actions - or as she later described it, her personal crusade.

A working-class girl from one of the roughest parts of the east-end of London, she had made a lot of money at an early age through various nefarious activities. And for nefarious, read, not just illegal - but, very illegal.

She produced high quality fake documents - evidence of her exceptional eyesight, skill and attention to detail.

That led to frequent contact with many of London's criminal gangs who learned to respect not just the documents she produced, but also her toughness.

She never backed away from an argument and always made her customers pay for the goods she supplied.

As a result, she earned respect and a great many friends.

She also thought she could take care of herself.

So, with her bold humanitarian agenda, she created

hundreds of false Identity papers with the intention of saving the women and children being persecuted by Boko Haram.

Price recalled a conversation months after she had left Africa, where she said, "An orphaned child in the UK is still better than one who's being raped and used as a human shield by those sick bastards."

He didn't disagree. The problem, however, was that she had become emotionally involved - something that Price always tried to avoid when carrying out his duties for SIS.

As he related to her some years later. "It blurs your judgement. For anyone with a conscience, it's also one of the recurring challenges you have to confront when working undercover. Over the years, it's the reason that many people have lost their lives. They get too involved, they lose their objectivity and as a direct result, they inevitably take unnecessary risks."

Fortunately, or unfortunately, Grandma had enjoyed a lot of early success - mostly, Price noted, the result of pure blind luck.

Some of the children had become very sick and were spreading infections amongst the Boko Haram leaders. So, whilst posing as a humanitarian aid worker, she had managed to guide almost a hundred of them to a nearby United Nations camp - discretely providing them with UK passports and identification papers at the same time.

From her perspective, the same negotiation skills that she'd employed with criminal gangs in London's east end, had secured their freedom - in exchange for the promise of medicine.

Grandma knew that Boko Haram did not officially permit their people to receive modern medical care. However, she also knew that like most terrorists, they were hypocrites.

They needed to survive. So, the offer of modern drugs had been gladly accepted - albeit, unofficially and with the usual accompaniment of death threats.

Ignoring the death threats, it unfortunately meant that Grandma had grown over-confident. She had failed to realise that they had followed her and discovered her real motives.

Consequently, when she had returned to the Boko Haram camp for a second time, to see how many children were left, they were waiting for her.

Stories of her bravery had reached SIS very quickly.

The British Embassy staff had been monitoring the situation locally and reported that she was being held against her will.

After further investigations, they managed to locate her. She was locked in a small one-story building on the outskirts of Baga - a town in the far north east of Nigeria and a well-known Boko Haram stronghold.

Price recalled that her escape had been brave and, in the best traditions of escapes - entirely opportunistic.

Grandma had been cowering in the corner of a small room, whilst a gang of the killers told her how they were going to rape her, before torturing and killing her later the same evening. Then their leader had appeared with a young woman he had already abused, and told them to enjoy themselves.

The gang had started cheering - dragging the woman outside, despite her screams of terror.

Unbelievably, and to Grandma's surprise, in their deranged excitement they had accidentally left the door unlocked.

Grandma, hardly believing her luck, had walked outside. Then glancing around in amazement, she grabbed an AK47 that was propped up against a wall on the way out of the camp.

Price remembered that it was her emotion - or as he preferred to think of it, her spirit - that was nearly her undoing.

As she ran out of the camp, she saw the young woman stark naked - bent forward over a wall, as she was abused from behind - whilst a queue of terrorists stood in line with their trousers around their ankles, waiting for their turn.

Price remembered her describing how, just looking at the horrific scene made her feel sick. And how she had felt compelled to raise the AK47, grip it as tightly as she possibly could and gently pull the trigger.

She killed the entire line of terrorists in one go, before fleeing in to the jungle.

From the comfort of SIS's iconic headquarters in London, Price remembered the satellite images and the Chief's words.

He had said, "That may have been a mistake. She may well come to regret that heroic display of humanity."

For his part, Price had just watched her sprint through the streets, alleyways and slums of Baga.

She had the gun slung over her shoulder and was periodically turning and firing a burst of bullets at the gang who were following her.

Assisted by the US, a drone had been sent in to follow her progress - displaying more detailed and often disturbing images, as she fled for her life.

In the end, it was only as a result of her crawling through a sewage pipe, that she had managed to evade capture. Although, it was very clear that the effects of the sewage had taken their toll. She was seen laying in a pile of effluent - coughing and vomiting.

SIS's medical experts were absolutely certain that her days were numbered and that she would be lucky to survive for more than a day or two.

A hastily prepared plan had been formed to extract her. Price even recalled the Chief's final words as he boarded a Royal Air Force transport plane.

"If they capture her, we'll abort," he had said. "There's no point in putting you at risk to rescue a dead body."

Eight hours later though, coordinates had flashed on Price's handheld GPS tracker. It had been the middle of the night and it appeared that she had managed to crawl away from the sewage and evade capture by hiding in a creak at the side of a tributary from Lake Chad.

The images from the US drone had made depressing viewing though. Not only was she still vomiting, she had been shot in one arm and was bleeding badly.

Price recalled the plane door opening as he rechecked his equipment and waited for the green light before jumping in to the darkness.

Thinking back to his feelings at the time, Price smiled. A night jump was a jump in to an abyss - something he always enjoyed. It was a lot more extreme, but in some ways similar to the first time he took a breath underwater whilst learning to scuba dive.

It was test of faith. Faith in the people who trained him and faith in the equipment itself.

That particular jump had been at high-altitude. A so-called HALO jump to avoid being seen by the local authorities as well as the terrorists.

In parallel, two Typhoon jet fighters that had been carrying out a training exercise off the coast of Africa, had taken off from Britain's Royal Air Force base on Ascension Island.

Price remembered that the extraction had been relatively straightforward. Indeed, he hadn't fired a single shot, which he always regarded as a measure of success.

Grandma had been sitting with her arms wrapped around herself, shivering at the bottom of a ditch when he'd arrived at her location.

Fortunately, there had been nobody else around. So, he had announced himself from a distance - relying on his British accident and some personal information from a background check on her, to identify him as a friend.

From there, after quickly treating her wounds and giving her a drink, they had walked around two miles in total darkness - arm-in-arm, relying on Price's night vision goggles and radio updates from the US drone flying overhead, to guide them.

A stolen jeep and a few hours later, they were being flown at supersonic speeds as the Typhoons spirited them towards Ascension Island and home.

Price parked his car a few hundred yards away from Grandma's house, remembering the extraordinary acceleration of the jets as they took off from Maiduguri International Airport.

The operation had been coordinated with the Nigerian government. However, nobody had been surprised to hear the sound of AK47 rounds ring out as the planes climbed away from the runway.

There were terrorists everywhere in that region of Nigeria.

Price recalled thinking the pilots were fearless as they sped south west at supersonic speeds - undeterred by gunfire, at times less than a hundred feet above the ground.

It had been whilst sitting in the back of a Royal Air Force transport plane, during the long flight from Ascension Island back to London, that Grandma had explained her nickname and he had discovered that they shared a mutual friend - the same mutual friend who had provided Grandma with all the intelligence information she had needed to carry out her personal crusade.

Price used the back of his hand to wipe a tear away from his eye as he remembered her - slowly walking towards Grandma's house, staying in the shadows whilst also reporting his arrival to the MI5 team of watchers who updated the Chief of Staff at SIS headquarters.

Price's earpiece beeped as an MI5 watcher spoke, "Stay back. She's on the phone and looking out of the window."

Price stopped and ducked in to a door way as he replied, "Do we know who?"

"No. GCHQ are attempting to listen in. It's encrypted though. May take a while."

"OK."

Inside the house, it had been Grandma who initiated the call.

"Hello, it's me."

The voice on the other end of the line was disguised by a computer, so it was impossible to determine who was speaking, or even make out their gender.

It said, "Keep it brief."

"He just called me as you said he would. We met and he wants a passport and a matching credit card tomorrow."

"I assume you agreed?"

"Yes."

"What name will you give him?"

"D'you really need that?"

"Yes."

"Why d'you need it? I feel bad even telling you about this."

"The name please!"

"OK. OK. He'll be Peter Nowak. That's N O W A K."

"Thank you."

"But you gotta promise me nothing'll happen to him while he's still in London. I got my reputation to think of. And he'll never know I told you, right?"

"Correct. He'll never know. And, once he's safely outside the UK, your account will be credited very generously in the usual way."

"Yeah, right. Thanks."

The line went dead as the person on the other end of the phone smiled - thinking, "He's on his way."

Price's earpiece beeped again, followed by, "She's off the phone."

"Thanks."

Price dialled her number, wondering if she would answer as he was hiding his number.

"Hello?"

"Good evening, it's me," Price replied - attempting a happy, almost jovial tone of voice.

"Hello, this is an unexpected surprise. What can I do for you?"

"Busy?"

Grandma hesitated, "Why?"

"Are you busy? A rush job by any chance?"

"Yeah. But that's none of your business love. Sorry."

"That's fine. I just wondered if you were free for dinner?"

"Yeah. But not tonight. I'm sorry, I've got to get this done."

"No problem. We can do dinner once that's done. Or maybe lunch? Tomorrow perhaps?"

"I can't do tomorrow lunchtime. But I could do dinner."

"So, the handover is tomorrow lunchtime," Price thought to himself, before saying, "OK. So, maybe tomorrow night then. I'll call and reconfirm if that's OK?"

"Thanks. Sorry love."

"It's fine. Take care. Bye."

Price smiled as he disconnected the call, which he'd made whilst walking down a small alleyway behind her house.

It was completely unlit and conveniently, provided access to the rear of multiple properties that backed on to it - including, as it turned out, Grandma's kitchen.

Price retrieved a lock picking tool from his pocket and used it to dislodge the latch on her kitchen window, before very carefully sliding it open and climbing through.

"She's one of an increasingly rare breed," he reflected. "A source of reliable illegal passports. A very special lady indeed."

He had chosen the kitchen window rather than the door, because the latch was not secure and enabled him to unlock it without causing any damage - plus, the lights were out, so he assumed she was in one of the other rooms.

However, much to his surprise, as soon as he had climbed through the window and was facing the kitchen door, the light switched on.

Standing in the doorway was Grandma - holding a sawn-off shotgun.

"Why can't you just use the door Price. You know, like normal people do?"

"There's a rather violent Russian agent somewhere out there. I wanted to avoid being seen."

"Plus, half of your Security Service I suppose?"

Price smiled, "There maybe one or two people from our lovely MI5 as well. That is true."

"I hope he hasn't seen them."

"I told them to be careful, don't worry. Actually, I had thought of asking you to help me get the Russian."

"No chance love. You know I have my reputation to think of. Which means, don't you go touching 'im until he's long gone, OK?"

"Of course, Grandma."

Grandma suddenly moved, far more swiftly than Price had expected.

In a fraction of a second, she was holding the sawn-off shotgun - the legendary device used by gangsters of years gone by - inches from his face.

Price smiled as he examined the end of the gun barrel.

He could see where it had been shortened, thereby removing the choke, which would normally help to contain the shot to improve accuracy at a distance. Whereas now, in its modified state, he was well aware that if Grandma pulled the trigger, the shot would erupt more as a mist.

"Although," he reflected, "At this close range, I've had it either way - sawn-off or otherwise."

"That's very old-fashioned," he remarked - attempting to diffuse the situation.

"It's served me well this old gun. I'm tellin' you Price. You let 'im go or I'll send you home with a hole or two in places where you don't want 'em."

"Grandma, I promise he won't be touched until he leaves the country. Now please, can we have a cup of tea?"

Part of Price's brain was telling him to disarm the lady and make her tell him exactly where she was handing over the passport to Slavic Stepka.

However, he also knew that would be very foolish.

Yes, with his training he could do that quite easily. But she had friends - a lot of friends. And thinking back to his training, he could hear the instructor saying, "Play the long game Price. Don't make the mistake of going for the short-term win. Word always gets out, and eventually it will be you with a target on your back."

Price knew it had been good advice. He'd seen colleagues do some inconceivable things under stress. He'd seen people inflict horrific pain - torturing and even killing innocent people.

It never ended well. In the end, the victims would say anything for the pain to stop - often inventing stories that created even more havoc.

Grandma seemed to read his thoughts as she turned, walked away and stowed the shotgun in its cupboard.

Looking back at Price from across the room, she said, "Why d'you let me get away with that?"

Price shrugged his shoulders. "I'm not about to let a maniac like Slavic Stepka lose me a friend, because we both know that's who we are talking about."

Then, by way of a demonstration of his friendship and trust, Price walked across the kitchen - filling up the kettle with water - in the process, turning his back on Grandma.

As he switched it on, Price, still not facing Grandma, said, "There's a saying in the intelligence community. If Grandma gets you a passport, you are safe - at least, you are for a while. Your passports never get rejected. It's incredible."

Grandma casually walked to the fridge and took out a bottle of milk.

"That's because I'm very thorough Price. It's not just a document. It's a document that is properly recorded on all the government systems."

"I guess that's why it's so expensive," Price joked.

"You get what you pay for love."

"That's very true."

Then, turning to face Grandma he continued, "He won't be touched whilst he's in the UK. But we would like to follow him out of the country, which means we do need to know where he is going to be. Please?"

"Are we being listened to?"

Price thought for a moment, then reached in to his pocket and switched off his mobile phone - placing it on the kitchen table for Grandma to see.

"No. It's just you and me. I give you my word."

Grandma smiled, "That's only the second time you have ever said that to me."

"Really? I'm not sure I can remember the first time to be honest."

"It was in that ditch you pulled me out of in Africa. You identified yourself and told me to trust you. You gave me your word. That was what you said. They were your exact words. You asked me to take a leap of faith. And I guess I made that leap."

Price smiled, "Well I'm very glad you did. I meant it then and I mean it now."

Grandma nodded agreement. "I know that love. The handover is midday tomorrow. Whitechapel shelter for the homeless. Just make sure he's abroad before you go after him."

"You already have my word on that."

"He's evil you know."

Price nodded, "I know. You're not the first person to tell me that."

"Why do you do this? He could kill you. I know you're good at what you do Price. But so is he."

Price finished making the tea and handed Grandma a cup

whilst taking a sip of tea himself.

"It's funny you say that. Recent events have made me wonder if I should keep doing this you know. Maybe I've seen too many people die. Maybe it's time to do something else - to quit and go and settle down. Have sex, raise kids and get old gracefully."

Grandma laughed, "You chose a tough business Price. Spying is not easy and even now - when we're not at war with anyone - it's still punishable by death in most countries."

Price just nodded, as the room fell silent for a few seconds as both Price and Grandma just looked at each other - deep in thought.

Grandma eventually broke the silence.

"You know something? You never told me why you left the Paras. You're a very good soldier. Arguably a better soldier than a spy."

Then, realising she'd just criticised him, she added, "Sorry love."

Price smiled, as he knew she was right. He wasn't a particularly subtle individual - something that is just one of the many characteristics a good spy requires.

"It's a long story," he replied.

Grandma glanced at her watch. "We don't have hours, because, as I'm sure you know, I have a passport and credit card to sort out. But?"

Price laughed. He always enjoyed the honesty of their relationship - as well as all their long conversations.

"It was towards the end of the last Gulf War," he said. "Six of us had parachuted in to Iraq. The SAS were already in there. They just needed a bit more firepower to support them, and that was us. We landed armed to the teeth."

"The war wasn't over then?"

"No, there was still quite a bit of fighting in some areas. Which is why we'd set up a secret forward operating base that was supposed to be a safe zone for the SAS and other friendly special forces to re-equip themselves. It even had a small runway.

The problem was, a bunch of the Iraqi Republican Guards has discovered it. It was in the middle of nowhere. We don't know how they found us. But anyway, they did and very quickly they surrounded us and started attacking."

"What did you do?"

"There were two or three hundred of them and about a dozen of us and we were running low on ammo. Despite that, the SAS were brutal. I've never seen anything like it. They must have taken out a hundred with mortars and gunfire, plus a whole load of others in hand-to-hand fighting in the pitch black of the middle of the night.

We called in air support and the US and RAF bombed the crap out of the Iraqis. But they got reinforcements and we eventually started losing people.

On the fateful day, we were down to just three - two SAS guys and me.

Anyway, someone came up with an evacuation plan. Since we had a runway, three Tornado fighters touched down in the middle of the night - each with a vacant seat in the back."

"I seem to recall you telling me that you tested out for the air force, didn't you?"

"It's true, my first choice was to fly the planes. But when that didn't work out - something about me being too big for the ejector seats - I decided to jump out of them instead. Hence, the Paras."

"I'm not sure I really follow that logic - but fair enough. You made it out. That's what matters."

"Yeah, we got out of range of their guns pretty quickly. The pilots were flying extremely fast and low to avoid being seen. Then I heard on the radio that there was a small town nearby where more of the Republican Guards were still holding out - including the people that had supplied the soldiers who attacked us.

We didn't have any weapons on the fighters because all the weight was being consumed by long-range fuel tanks. So, we came up with an ambitious plan."

Grandma didn't reply. She waited as Price composed himself - he was clearly feeling emotional about the whole incident.

"The Tornado is, or rather was, one of the few fighters in the world that can fly supersonic at sea level. It was so well made, pretty much nothing slowed it down.

So, at my suggestion - my direction if I'm honest, as I did outrank the pilot at the time - the pilot set the TFR to fifty feet and aimed for the Republican Guard compound."

"TFR?"

"Terrain Following Radar. You set the height you want to fly above the ground and the radar scans ahead and keeps you safe. It stops you flying in to a mountain or a building by automatically adjusting your altitude."

"Oh really? So, low-flying is actually quite easy then," Grandma joked.

Price smiled. "It really isn't. Fast jet fighter pilots have nerves of steel, as well as being completely mad."

"I believe it's called bravery love."

"Well, whatever you call it," Price replied. "He set the height, swept the adjustable wings back and pushed the throttle forward to the maximum."

"How fast were you going?"

"According to the court martial, quite unbelievably, we were approaching Mach Two, when I dropped one of the auxiliary fuel tanks."

"Court martial?"

"I dropped the fuel tank on the Republican Guard compound. It was a good shot, if I say so myself. Not easy at that speed.

It exploded on impact and wiped out their accommodation block killing everyone inside - added to which, it was followed by a massive shockwave due to our speed. That did a fair amount of damage as well."

Grandma laughed. "They got the message then. And well done you. I did tell you you're a good soldier. You deserved a medal."

"Well that's the irony I suppose. I got a medal for the

earlier fight with the SAS. But the attack on the compound was deemed illegal. It broke the rules of engagement and tragically killed a bunch of innocent civilians who happened to be there along with the soldiers.

The whole thing was my idea so, as you'd expect, I insisted on taking the blame - although, with respect to the pilot, he repeatedly objected.

Anyway, the judgement was not a surprise. They decided that as a result of my order to the pilot, I should be dishonourably discharged from the Paras. And they would have got their way if the SIS Chief hadn't saved me.

I'd been doing some intelligence work for the army some months earlier, and I guess I must have made an impression, because he stepped in and saved my neck."

Price smiled as he added, "Rumour has it, he called in a few favours. Apparently, he made some not very subtle references to pictures of senior officers doing things their wives, and in some cases the police, wouldn't appreciate. Needless to say, they cooperated and I was transferred to SIS, where I've been ever since."

Grandma laughed. "That shows how important it is to have friends love. You know that as well as I do."

Price nodded agreement as Grandma added, "And you got the bastards that killed your friends. As far as I'm concerned, that's what counts."

"Yeah, but the damage was far worse than I had expected. The satellite images before and after said it all. Frankly, given the devastation we caused, I think I would have fired me."

"They killed your friends and colleagues."

"And that's why I don't regret it. But that's not a valid reason Grandma. You know that as well as I do."

"Yeah well. I would have done the same thing if I'd been given the opportunity. So, don't go feeling bad, alright?"

Price smiled. "I know. I miss our chats you know. We should keep in touch more regularly."

Grandma smiled, as she'd been thinking exactly the same thing. Then, after a brief moment of silence, she asked, "How's Mary by the way?"

Price walked forward and put his arms around his old friend as he said, "She was killed whilst working. I'm so sorry. It's awful."

Grandma pushed Price away and stared at him with an almost cold expression. She knew how close Price and Mary were and could see tears forming in his eyes.

"Go home Price," she said as she turned away from him. "Don't be so upset. It's the life she chose - just the same as you."

Price was stunned the sudden cold assertiveness. He couldn't understand it - it was as if he had offended her.

He'd been expecting words of comfort. But it was very clear they weren't arriving any time soon.

So, after a brief pause he said, "Yes of course. I'm so sorry. I shouldn't have disturbed you."

Then, picking up his mobile phone, he left by the kitchen's backdoor.

14. On The Road

There are over six-hundred thousand CCTV cameras in London that monitor almost every aspect of life across, in and under the city.

Many of these are linked to databases and enable the police and security services to almost instantaneously identify people as they come and go.

The vast majority are of the information is discarded of course, as it's just decent people going about their lives. However, when there's a criminal on the move, it can be extremely useful - something that Price was more than happy to take advantage of - in this case, watching events unfold from the relative calm of the SIS operations room.

A few miles away in Whitechapel, his colleagues from MI5 were taking a more direct approach. Intelligence officers were strategically located at various intervals along the route they expected Grandma to take.

As he watched the CCTV monitors, Price recalled the Chief of Staff's remarks earlier in the day. He'd said, "We'll follow her, find him, let him get out of the country and you finish the job. Ideally do the job discreetly. But, if that's not possible, just make sure you don't get caught, as this is not official."

Snapping his thoughts back to the present, Price watched Grandma step off a train in Whitechapel underground station and spoke in to his headset to update the MI5 team.

181

"She'll be arriving in two minutes. Grey jacket, blue faded jeans and a brown head scarf that's seen better days."

The computer screen in front of him, lit up as the various officers silently signalled their receipt of the message and coordinated their movements - each one handing off to the next as Grandma walked along the road - thereby ensuring that no individual spent sufficient time following her for it to become suspicious.

As Grandma approached the shelter for the homeless, she disappeared from the CCTV cameras.

For a brief moment, the nervousness of the moment made Price's heart skip a beat.

He needn't have worried though. A few seconds later the computer screen lit up once again, indicating the handover was successful and that Slavic Stepka had been positively identified.

Shortly afterwards a message appeared:

SUBJECT IN BEIGE TOYOTA CAMRY

Price smiled as he turned to one of the operations room staff. It was a colleague he had worked with many times before - on several occasions relying on his guidance whilst operating in hostile territories abroad.

"They're very good at this, aren't they Adam?"

Adam looked up and smiled as he said, "That they are Sir. I have the car's number plate now as well. We've got him. He's ours. We can track him anywhere."

The words, "Don't be so sure," kept going through Price's head. Immediately followed by, "This is way too easy. And what a fantastic coincidence it was Grandma providing the passport."

On reflection, he decided that it could not have been a coincidence - it was nothing less than damned suspicious.

Price stared intently at the CCTV and traffic cameras, as the Toyota Camry driven by Slavic Stepka made its way through the streets of east London.

"Are any of the Five officers armed," he asked the Chief of Staff.

"Unlikely. Why?"

Price gave a shrug of his shoulders as he said, "I can't help thinking that someone should just shoot him in the head before he vanishes. I know the team from Five have got him covered for now. But I bet he will disappear soon. I would put money on it."

For a brief second, Price made eye contact with the Chief of Staff who didn't reply - indicating he shared Price's concern.

Turning his attention back to the computer screen, Price asked, "Has he got a mobile phone on him?"

"Too early to tell Sir," replied Adam. "There are so many people nearby that are all heading in the same direction. Give him a few minutes. We need him to change cell a few more times and take a couple of turns. Then we'll know for certain."

Price was about to speak again, when the Chief of Staff interrupted him - having clearly read his thoughts.

"Before you say it Price, no. We are not sending someone

down there to shoot him. We need to have evidence. Then we can arrest him and charge him. You know how it works in this country."

"But killing him in someone else's country is fine of course," Price muttered - mostly to himself.

"What was that you said?" asked the Chief of Staff.

"Sir, he killed dozens of people in the restaurant and the hotel. And here he is. A free man."

"We have no evidence it was him."

"Mary told me it was him."

The Chief of Staff laughed. "You're referring to a statement from an agent who is not only dead, but happens to work for a foreign power - and not a particularly friendly one at that."

Price made eye contact with the Chief of Staff but didn't speak.

"Sorry. I didn't mean to remind you of bad memories Price. But I'm sure you understand. Now, focus on the situation at hand please."

Price nodded. He fully understood, but his thoughts were interrupted as he watched the Toyota Camry slow down, pull over to the side of the road and park.

Price wasn't prone to angry outbursts and was often heard to proudly proclaim that he didn't hate anyone. However, as he watched Slavic Stepka get out of the car and walk in to a bookshop, he wished he was there.

He knew he'd given Grandma his word. But, armed or not, if he had been there, Slavic Stepka would only be leaving the bookshop one way. In a body bag.

Glancing down at his computer screen, Price was pleased to see the MI5 officers' communications. Two had the front covered, two were making their way behind the bookshop, another was inbound and would go in to the shop, whilst two more were waiting for him to exit, covering both directions in case he made a U-turn.

Suddenly, as he continued to watch the CCTV, Price saw smoke coming from his car.

"Car's on fire," he announced to the MI5 team. "This will be a deliberate diversion. Don't let it distract you," as the Chief of Staff alerted the Police and the London Fire Service.

Price couldn't care less about the car. His instincts told him that this was where Slavic Stepka would vanish. So, he spoke again.

"Team, I reckon this is where it happens. This is where he tries to lose us. This guy is not an amateur. Get eyes on him now please."

One of the MI5 team spoke for the first time. "But Sir, we have an agreed strategy for this scenario."

"I don't care! Get in there now and make sure you can see him. I don't care how - just make up an excuse!"

"But Sir?"

The Chief of Staff interrupted, "I am operational lead here. Get in there now. I want confirmation of visual contact."

Price didn't acknowledge the Chief of Staff. Such was their

relationship, they both knew it wasn't necessary. They just watched as four intelligence officers entered the bookshop.

Then, as the car started to burn more furiously, sending clouds of smoke in to the air, one of the MI5 officers ran out of the book shop, straight in to the road.

He was shouting in to his headset, "The pub. The pub," as he sprinted across the busy road - narrowly missing cars that screeched to a halt to avoid an accident.

As he made it to the other side of the road, another MI5 officer, who'd remained in the bookshop, said, "He's not in here. He's gone. There's an underground tunnel that links the shop to the pub."

Price glanced over at Adam who was typing furiously on his computer. Then, after a brief pause Adam said, "That's correct Sir. It dates back to when the book shop was a pub as well. It would be well over forty years ago. It must have been a convenient way to get beer between the two buildings. It's actually quite common where there are two pubs close to each other."

Price cursed, as he heard another MI5 officer declare, "He's not in the pub Sir. I just went through the tunnel. I'm standing in the pub as we speak and the door is open. He's gone. I repeat, he has gone!"

"CCTV behind that pub?" the Chief of Staff asked.

Adam nodded no. "There's nothing around there Sir. But I have a list of car registration plates from the traffic cameras nearby. He's bound to have switched vehicles. I'll map that to the cell phones that were in the area when he received the package and see if there's any correlation."

Price made eye contact with the Chief of Staff, who said, "He planned that very well."

Price just nodded in agreement as the room fell silent, whilst they all watched the fire in the Toyota being extinguished.

Twenty minutes later, however, Adam broke the silence.

"OK gents, we have three vehicles of interest. A small red Ford Fiesta, a blue Toyota 4x4 and a blue-and-orange motorbike. I reckon our target is in the Ford. And he's made very good ground. He's clearly put the hammer down, because he's already heading out of London with the other two not far behind."

Price was about to speak, when Adam added, "Here's the traffic camera footage," as he switched the image on the main screen in the operations room to show motorway traffic, highlighting the three vehicles in the process.

"Here's a dumb question. Given that the other two are not us, do we have any idea who the hell they are?" Price asked.

Adam's expression was one of concern as he turned to Price.

"No. We could check their passports at the border, but that would make them suspicious. If they're pros they'll know how it works just as well as we do."

"So, we have no idea why they're following him? The plates don't give us any clue at all?"

Adam looked back down at the computer. "Nothing useful

yet Sir. The 4x4 is owned by some Welsh guy who isn't answering his phone. The chances are it's probably stolen and he hasn't reported it yet, because his mobile is still in Wales. No idea about the bike yet either. It appears to be brand new and registered to an accounting firm in Yorkshire.

Both local police forces have been notified. They're sending uniformed officers over to both the Welsh guy and the accounting firm."

Price looked at the Chief of Staff.

"In the absence of any other information, I'm guessing they're either protection for him from us or they're Russians out to eliminate him. Either way, we don't have enough evidence to stop them at this stage. It's all pure conjecture. They might even be completely innocent and just happen to be going in the same direction."

The Chief of Staff agreed, "The 4x4 could even be the Welsh guy who just happened to forget his phone, for all we know. We can't stop them without reasonable cause. We'll just have to let them go and wait and see if they make some kind of a move."

Price conceded, "It is what it is. If they are out to get him, I'm guessing they'll make their move once they're stationary and crossing the Channel."

Price was about to continue speaking, when Adam interrupted them again. "Bad news. The 4x4 is gaining on the Ford. Here's a close-up Sir."

"Alert the police. We need an armed response unit," the Chief of Staff ordered, as they watched the passenger in the front of the 4x4 leaned out of the window - clearly aiming a gun forward.

Then suddenly, the motorbike appeared almost from nowhere - having been nearly a mile behind the other vehicles.

They all watched as it easily drew level with the 4x4, such was its incredible speed. Then, to their horror, they noticed that the rider was holding a weapon and was pointing it at the underside of the vehicle.

Price recognised it in an instant.

"That looks like a mini grenade launcher fitted to an MP5." Then, remembering his own use of exactly the same weapon, he laughed and said, "This will not end well. At least, not for the 4x4 if that biker fires now."

The biker did fire - almost immediately. Two shots in quick succession - perfectly timed and with pinpoint accuracy so that the explosive shells detonated under the middle of the 4x4's body with devastating effect.

The fireball burst upwards and outwards from under the vehicle, flipping the 4x4 over as if it were as light as a feather.

As it tumbled down the motorway, rolling over again and again engulfed in flames, it began to break apart, sending fragments of metal and body panels across the road - in the process hurling one of the passengers across the dual carriageway and into oncoming traffic.

Whilst being horrified by the scene before him, Price couldn't help smiling to himself as he noted how his priorities differed from those of the Chief of Staff.

He turned to Adam and said, "Keep tracking the Ford and

the bike. Do not lose them."

Adam nodded his acknowledgement - whilst in parallel, the Chief of Staff said, "Alert the fire and ambulance services. We'll need to close the road in both directions to help the wounded and gather evidence."

The phone next to the Chief of Staff interrupted them.

After a brief conversation, he turned to Price and said, "GCHQ are seeing increased communications traffic. Russian communications traffic. It looks like it was them and they're sending another team."

"Wow! Stepka really did manage to piss them off," Price joked.

Before anyone could speak again, Adam said, "I've still got eyes on the Ford, but I'm sorry to report that the bike has vanished."

"What happened to it?"

"The rider is a maniac Sir. He rode up the grass banking at the side of the motorway and disappeared from view."

"Any news on the plates?"

Adam looked down at his computer screen and said, "Yes Sir. Police confirm the motorbike is owned by one of the partners in the accounting firm. Seems he's off work today. They're attempting to track him down via family and friends. As for the 4x4 - not that it really matters now - but Welsh police confirm it was stolen last night."

Then, whilst laughing he added, "It seems the owner had sneaked away for a couple of days with a young lady and didn't want his wife to find out, which is why it hadn't been reported earlier."

Price couldn't help smiling as he asked, "Has the biker got a mobile phone?"

"Earlier Sir, yes. But that number is no longer logged in to any cells."

"Smart," Price acknowledged. "Switched it off. That's what I would have done in the same situation."

"Absolutely Sir," Adam conceded.

"Alert the Channel Tunnel and the sea ports to look out for the bike anyway. I'm sure it will be pointless, but just in case."

"Why is it pointless Price?", the Chief of Staff asked,

"I would bet that's the killer from Bratislava. I don't know why. Maybe it's the precision - the professional way that hit was executed. It's just a hunch."

"And?"

"If I were him and I'd just executed a bunch of people in public like that, I'd make sure I was well hidden from prying eyes. And given that we already know he's good, I see no reason to believe he won't do exactly that."

Then after a short pause he added, "That said, we're all human and we all make mistakes sometimes. So, we have to check. It's the right thing to do."

"Why would he want to protect Slavic Stepka if he's also his target?"

"I don't know Sir. But it seems to me that Stepka's going to be protected for much of his journey - assuming we don't lose him again. So, I think I should get to Bratislava and deal with him there."

The Chief of Staff nodded agreement, just as Adam interrupted them again. "Sorry Sir, the Ford has gone as well - we've lost him. He's heading down country lanes where there are no cameras. Five are on their way."

Price walked to the door - turning at the last second to look back across the room as he was about to leave.

He said, "Gents, keep me updated please."

Then, he made his way to the rooftop helipad for the one hour journey to the UK's Royal Air Force base, Coningsby, in Lincolnshire.

As they touched down, Price's mobile phone buzzed. It was a message from the Chief of Staff, telling him that Slavic Stepka had been identified boarding Le Shuttle - the train that takes cars through the Channel Tunnel that links the UK to France and the rest of the European mainland.

Given the train schedule, that meant he would be through the tunnel in around thirty minutes and, provided he didn't make any stops along the way, could be in Bratislava in as little as twelve hours.

Keen to get ahead of him, Price changed in to a flying suit and shook hands with an old friend.

"Flight Lieutenant Parsons, a pleasure as always."

The air force officer smiled as he held out his arm to shake hands.

"Price, good to see you, old friend. I've been told to give you the ride of your life. French and German military air control have given us approval to fly supersonic - provided that is, we make sure we avoid the main population areas and stay at high altitude."

Price smiled back, "I'm looking forward to it. How long do you think it will take?"

"Just under an hour. I hear you need to get their very quickly. Our flight path takes us east out over the sea, before we turn towards the south east and then sit at Mach Two pretty much all the way there."

Pointing to Price's rucksack, he said, "Come on, grab your bag. Let's get going."

As they boarded the two-seater variant of the Typhoon fighter jet, Price smiled, remembering his last flight in the same aircraft. A smile that became a laugh as the engines' afterburners powered up and he felt the extraordinary thrust of acceleration as the jet soared in to the sky.

Sure enough, just under an hour and a short taxi ride later, Price was in central Bratislava.

He closed his eyes to relax, as he sat by the window of the small apartment that had been arranged for him by the SIS station head for Eastern Europe.

Many years before it would have been part of a grand mansion - a key building in the historic central district of Bratislava. The beautiful stonework, clear evidence of its history that dated back to the nineteenth century.

More significantly for Price, however, it faced Hotel Duetel - the hotel where Slavic Stepka's sister and family were living with twenty-four-hour protection, whilst their own home was being rebuilt.

That was for another day though, because Price knew that Slavic Stepka would not be arriving any time soon. Most likely, he'd arrive the next day, given that he would need to refuel and probably get some rest at some point.

Price made himself some dinner - grateful that the fridge in the apartment had been left full of food.

Then, a couple of hours later his phoned beeped, with the message he had been waiting for.

Pressing the PLAY button on his mobile phone, Price thought, "The question is, where's his head? What has happened to Stepka between then and now?"

A female voice started to speak.

It was clear and concise - spoken with no emotion and phrased as a set of facts without judgement, so that Price could form his own opinion.

It described the events that had taken place as Slavic Stepka travelled through France and Belgium.

15:00 GMT: Target boards Le Shuttle train driving a grey transit van. No evidence based on the height and weight of the van that it contains significant freight, other than the driver. Although, there was something in the back. We think, possibly a small motorbike.

15:40 GMT: French police confirm arrival. Target appears to be heading for the Belgium border.

16:00 GMT: Belgium traffic police report seeing the transit van on the A14 travelling east.

16:50 GMT: Target transfers to the E40, still heading east as expected. ETA Bratislava at current speed is thirteen hours twenty-two minutes, assuming that the driver does not stop for a break to sleep.

18:00 GMT: Target has entered a motorway service station, presumably for fuel.

18:05 GMT: Black Toyota 4x4 - later identified as a stolen vehicle - enters slip road to the service station but stops short. Four people get out. They are all armed with machine pistols and start to walk towards Target's vehicle.

18:06 GMT: The four armed individuals begin to fire their weapons. The fire power is consistent, rapid and aimed directly at Target.

Price picked up the coffee mug he had rested on a table next to him - taking a sip as the voice continued.

18:07 GMT: Target appears unharmed and takes cover behind a large concrete pillar.

18:08 GMT: The four armed individuals start to walk further forward, suppressing any retaliatory action with more rapid fire.

18:09 GMT: Firing pauses whilst all four reload their weapons.

"That was a mistake. They should have staggered their reloading. They may regret that," thought Price, as the voice continued to speak.

18:10 Target reappears almost immediately. Target is now armed with a sub machine gun and runs north, away from the pumps. Target is firing whilst running. Two individuals from the 4x4 are killed instantly.

Price smiled to himself - thinking, "Told you."

18:11 GMT: Remaining two individuals run forward whilst firing bullets randomly in all directions. Pumps are now on fire. Explosions are starting to wreck cars. Bystanders are abandoning their vehicles and running for cover amid general chaos. The fire is spreading to the service station building itself.

18:12 GMT: Target fires a single shot from behind an out-building on the north side of the service station. One more individual from the 4x4 is killed. Only one remaining now.

18:13 GMT: Remaining individual runs in a zig-zag type movement towards Target, apparently unaware that Target has moved again.

18:14 GMT: Target emerges from behind a parked car. Target fires two shots but they both miss.

18:15 GMT: Both individuals start running between burning cars and petrol pumps. Judging by the pattern of movement, they are attempting to outflank each other and gain the upper hand. Then, suddenly they find themselves face-to-face. Target appears to fire his weapon at point-blank range. However, it is out of ammunition.

18:16 GMT: For several seconds, they appear to be having a conversation. We have not been able to ascertain what was said. Then the individual from the 4x4 raises his weapon - presumably to fire at Target.

18:17 GMT: Recording from nearby traffic cameras pick up a loud crack - later identified as the sound from a high-calibre sniper's rifle. 4x4 individual's head bursts apart sending blood in all directions. The body collapses to the floor in front of Target

18:18 GMT: Target retrieves a motorbike from the transit van and flees the scene.

18:20 GMT: Target transfers to small roads making it impossible to track via CCTV. No further sightings have been reported. It is highly likely, given the small engine size and off-road style of the motorbike, that Target has subsequently changed vehicle again, most likely to another car.

18:30 GMT: Further analysis of nearby traffic camera recordings identifies the sniper as a motorbike rider. Dimension analysis indicates it is likely the same biker that executed the occupants of a Toyota 4x4 in the U.K. earlier the same day. As yet, it has not been possible to trace the bike or the rider.

Price put his coffee down as the recording finished.

So that was the situation. Slavic Stepka's guardian angel had saved him again - whilst, quite possibly also being his murderer at some point in the future.

"Why," he thought. "Why save someone's life if you intend to kill them later? Aside from being a waste of time, it's also extremely risky. And, if the biker is the same person in black who had gone after the family, who the hell is he?"

Price finished his coffee not knowing the answers to his own questions. One thing was for sure though, the next day would be an unpleasant one - one that would be far safer if he had a better knowledge of his surroundings.

In theory, Price was hoping that he would be able to look

out at the street below, watch Slavic Stepka walk to the front of the hotel and execute him with a single silenced shot before he even knew Price was there.

Sure, the direction of the bullet would give away his location if observed by an expert. But, this was a hotel and Price knew that the initial panic and confusion would be more than sufficient for him to make a hasty exit in to the surrounding streets - well before a police cordon could be put in place.

However, experience had also taught him that it was never that simple - especially when the target was someone as experienced as Slavic Stepka.

With that in mind, Price picked up his mobile phone and, leaving his gun locked in the apartment, went for a walk around the streets, to get his bearings and plan his escape route.

A few hours and many streets later, Price found himself seated in a small bar, saying, "My name is Elliot. Yes, I'm from England."

And shortly after, "Really? You want champagne? Yes of course, I thought you might. Here's my credit card."

What Price didn't know was, across the room the manager of the bar was speaking quietly in to his mobile phone. And he was engaged in a very different conversation.

"He's in the hostess bar with a girl."

"What's he doing?"

"Drinking a cocktail. A Bloody Mary I think."

"What's he doing with the girl?"

"Why do you care?"

"Answer my question!"

"Nothing. They're just talking."

"What are they talking about?"

"He's pretending to be drunk by the sounds of it. He just asked the girl if she had a twin sister."

"Why pretending?"

"He's a very big guy. There's no way he could be drunk after only a couple of drinks."

"Don't let him out of your sight. Don't hurt him. But follow him. I want to know where he's staying."

"What if he sees us?"

"Don't be seen you fool!"

"OK."

"Maybe see if you can get the girl to get the address from him?"

"Yeah, good idea. I'll do that. They're very used to getting information out of people. And cash as well, actually."

Shortly after - whilst Price was visiting the bathroom and collecting a fresh drink - the manager told the girl to find out where he lived.

Consequently, when Price returned, much to his surprise, she was even more welcoming than she had been before. So much so, that he almost became suspicious.

As she threw her arms around him and kissed him on the cheek, Price gave her a disapproving look, then just smiled and raised his glass, so that she would back off slightly.

The girl pretended to look upset and offended, and then said, "Let's go back to your place. We can have some fun. Do you stay near here?"

Price nodded no, "I'm flattered miss, but I'm going home alone tonight."

"I'll just stay with you a short time," she whispered in his ear. "Just long enough to make you tired. "

Price laughed as he made eye contact with her and said, "Have another drink."

In the end, several hours later Price paid the bill and left on his own.

"Well?" asked the manager, as he towered over the girl.

"He's staying near here. It's not his home though. He walked here, but wouldn't tell me the address."

The manager's temper erupted, as he shouted, "You fucking whore! I gave you one job to do!"

The girl had worked in the bar for a few years and was used to his outbursts. She didn't react other than to add, "I told you, he's probably a tourist. I don't think he even knows the address. I think he's staying with a friend or something like that."

The manager, however, wasn't interested. He turned and walked away - immediately making a call with his mobile phone.

Price, meanwhile, walked casually along the dark cobbled-stone street in the early hours of the morning, blissfully unaware that he was now being followed.

His primary concern was finding his way through historic lanes between the old buildings which, in the middle of the night and after a few drinks, had a tendency to all look rather similar.

It was only as he stopped at a T-junction, desperately trying to remember whether to turn left or right that, by pure chance, he glanced across the road and saw the reflection of a figure in the glass front of a shop.

Seeing someone's reflection wasn't something he'd usually be concerned about. But when that person, at such an odd hour of the day, immediately ducks into an alcove at the side of the road - presumably to avoid being seen - it's clearly an issue.

Price cursed, regretting he'd even chosen to leave the apartment - whilst thinking, "How long has he been following me? Was he watching me in the bar? Was I drugged? Is he on his own or is there an entire team?"

The sudden realisation that he was potentially in danger, kicked Price's brain in to action, sending adrenaline surging through his body - in a small way, counteracting some of the effects of the alcohol.

He looked left and right, eventually remembering that the way back was to the right. So instead, he turned left - wishing that he had brought a weapon with him, as he was sure the person following would be armed.

That said, Price was also fairly sure his tail - or as he preferred to refer to him, his shadow - wouldn't make an aggressive move in a public street. A glance up at the side of the buildings made that extremely foolish. There were far too many CCTV cameras.

Price started looking for somewhere dark. He needed to find a place for confrontation - eventually noticing a small lane that provided a back entrance to two rows of restaurants.

Judging by the state of it, it also provided a convenient place to dump rubbish, as it was crammed full of trash cans, bags and cans of food waste, "And more than its fair share of rats no doubt," Price muttered to himself, as he calmly turned the corner - immediately sprinting in to almost total darkness - stopping around twenty yards later and hiding behind a large pile of trash.

Looking back to the main road, Price could see a large man. He created a tall silhouette against the amber colour of the streetlights in the distance.

As the man began to walk forward, Price opened his right eye. He had kept it closed for the previous few minutes so that it would be adjusted to the darkness.

Given the cloudy night sky and lack of moonlight, he hoped that it would give him a small advantage - if only a very brief one.

The man had drawn a pistol - what looked like a small 9mm Glock - although, in the darkness, it was difficult to be certain from the shape alone.

"So much for having a chat," Price thought, glancing down at his own hands. All he had was a piece of metal piping he'd found on the ground.

Around three feet long, it looked like part of some

construction material used in building scaffolding.

The man stepped a few feet to his right so that he was less visible - walking in shadows rather than the centre of the lane. He was clearly no amateur. Although, as he discovered almost immediately, that made it far more hazardous - as he kicked cardboard box full of discarded rubbish, disturbing a rat that immediately scurried away.

Price stood completely still - not reacting as the rat ran past his feet, clipping the end of his left shoe in the process. He just held the metal piping aloft - ready to strike.

He was sure the man couldn't see him. His eyes wouldn't have adjusted that quickly as Price could only see the man with one eye. That said, his left eye was also starting to adjust to the darkness, but wasn't quite there yet.

"Come on. Get a move on," he thought. "We need to get this started before our odds even out."

Suddenly, the man stopped.

Price knew why. He'd heard it as well. There had been movement further down the lane.

For a few seconds, nobody moved. Then, there it was again - a ruffling sound as another rat darted between bags of rubbish.

The man, realising what it was, resumed his steady pace down the lane - waiving his gun left and right as he searched for Price.

But Price wasn't about to let him get the advantage. He removed a small coin from his pocket and flicked it across the lane so that it struck the far wall.

For the tinniest traction of a second he saw the man's head move as his attention was briefly diverted - just as Price leapt forward, striking down with the metal pipe, smashing it across man's wrists as hard as he could.

The gun disappeared in to the darkness and Price was sure he'd broken the man's wrist. Certainly, he heard a crack as the man cried out in pain.

Price withdrew the metal pipe, intending to follow it with a second strike to the man's chest, in order to disable him long enough to try and find out who he was. Certainly, after such a violent initial blow, he was not expecting his opponent to be in any state to put up strong resistance.

However, much to his surprise, the man suddenly lunged forward using his weight and momentum to push Price backwards as he flung his arms around his neck and wrestled him to the ground - sending the metal pipe flying in to the darkness at the same time.

Price fell backwards - his head smashing in to a trash can, as he grabbed the man's neck with his left hand, in an attempt to complete a stranglehold of his own.

He could see the man's right hand was bleeding as he tightened his grip on the man's neck. but that didn't stop the man using his left arm - swinging it hard and landing a brutal punch to Price's face.

Price grimaced as the pain shot through his head. But it made no difference. He'd been hit before and just tightened his grip around the man's windpipe as he twisted and turned.

Another strike to the face, however, was even harder.

Price momentarily lost grip as he felt the man's knee

strike him in the stomach. The man's full weight now rested on to his chest.

Pinned down and in desperation Price reached out with his left hand - searching for any kind of weapon, just as the man landed a third brutal blow.

Price tried to defend his face with his right hand as another knee plunged in to his abdomen and a fist smashed down on him.

Then his hand found something. "Yes," he thought, as he grabbed it. It was a rock of some kind.

Without even thinking, Price smashed it down on the man's head as hard as he could.

The man cried out in pain, clutched his head and moved backwards - thereby removing some of the pressure on Price's chest.

Price knew that was his opportunity. He sat up, scrambled to his knees and flung himself forward, using his weight to push the man off-balance.

The man tried to move, but before he could, Price smashed the rock down again - except this time it was in to the man's right eye.

The man cried out and struggled to move as Price struck again, as hard as he could to the man's neck. Then again and again and again.

Price swore he heard a crack as the man's eyes filled with panic and fear. But that didn't stop him making a last desperate move - his left arm, reaching up and scratching Price's face.

Price instinctively pulled back in pain as blood flowed from his cheek. But he wasn't about to let the man escape. He raised his left arm one last time, and swung it down across the man's neck with a violent chopping movement.

The man stopped moving as Price sat back for a few moments to gather his strength.

He could feel blood pouring from his nose where he'd been punched and from the scratches on his face. But he didn't have time to worry about that. That would have to wait until he was back in the safety of the apartment.

A quick search of the man's pockets revealed nothing. Price wasn't surprised, as he thought, "Maybe we have him on file somewhere," as he took a secure photo using an SIS application installed on his mobile phone.

The problem he now faced, however, was DNA.

The man had scratched his face and drawn blood, which meant, aside from the blood on his clothes, on the man's clothes and on the ground, there would be skin fragments lodged under the nails of his fingers.

Price knew that, for any forensic team investigating the death, it would be impossible to avoid finding evidence, even if they weren't looking for it.

And, what they would find would be more than sufficient to convict him of murder.

Looking around, Price noticed a few cans with some used cooking oil - quickly realising there was only one answer to the problem.

As he poured the oil all over the man and the ground

where they had been fighting - covering the metal pipe he'd been holding earlier as well, for good measure - Price felt bad.

This wasn't how he would usually want to end someone's life. Even his enemies deserved some dignity in death.

He also knew that he had no choice.

So, Price reached in to his pocket, withdrew a cigarette lighter, flicked the switch, dropped it and walked away as the lane burst in to flames.

15. The Chase

Price was confident that he'd finally managed to get back to the apartment without being followed.

But it was at a cost. The bruises on his face hurt like hell, and looking in the mirror he could see why.

It wasn't a pretty sight.

Price re-read the message on his phone. It was the same message that woke him in the early hours of the morning, and was what he had been waiting for. Slavic Stepka had contacted his sister - he was on his way to see her.

A strong black coffee helped to bring some life back to his brain and his tired bruised face.

Glancing down at his mobile phone in case there were further messages, he moved a small chair - placing it in front of the old-fashioned sachet window. By opening it just a few inches, he managed to provide space for his MP5's suppressor that was now covered with a small blanket to disguise its true purpose.

It was still dark outside. The sun would take at least another few hours before it rose above the horizon. Nevertheless, looking across the wide road, Price could clearly see the front entrance of the hotel. It was lit on the outside by a tall street-light around twenty yards away - as well as from the inside by the impressive foyer.

The SIS station chief had informed Price that there were only two ways in to the building. There was the front entrance on the main road and a discrete service entrance, accessed via a small alleyway to the left of the building.

Price picked up his MP5 and switched the sight to infrared.

Whilst the service entrance was virtually impossible to see with just the light from the street - via infrared, he could make out the fine detail.

Nodding to himself, Price realised that if Slavic Stepka appeared by either entrance, he wouldn't stand a chance.

"It's just a matter of time," he thought, as he opened the SIS encrypted communications application on his phone and spoke in to his headset.

"Gamma four-two-four in position."

The Chief of Staff replied immediately, "He's in the city, but the CCTV cameras have lost sight of him."

Price sighed. "He seems to be very good at losing us. This is getting to be a habit. And not a good one."

"It's nothing you couldn't do in his position. Just be prepared to expect the unexpected."

"Roger that."

After a few seconds of total silence, the Chief of Staff added, "I can't believe he'll be dumb enough to just walk in the front door."

"He won't. That would be suicidal. He'll know that just as well as I do. He'll be up to something. He'll have an alternative way in that we haven't thought of yet. I'm sure of it. That's what makes this job so interesting."

"This is not a game Gamma four-two-four!"

Price almost laughed, whilst thinking that it was very much a game. A game of deviousness, determination and, for the moment, patience. However, he replied, "Of course not Sir. I'm just speculating as to how he's going to get in the building."

"How would you go in?"

"I'm not sure I would. Ordinarily, I would try and find a basement or a quiet entrance. But this place has nothing. I guess I might drop from the air - but there's no way he has the resources to arrange that. At least, not this quickly. So, in his position I'd probably make them come out, perhaps by setting off the fire alarm or creating a diversion of some kind."

"He could arrive by bus or something, so that you can't get a clear view of him."

"Yes," Price agreed, "But he still has to walk up the steps to the lobby. There's nearly a dozen steps and there's nothing in there to hide behind. I only need the smallest of gaps. Even if the first shot isn't fatal, as soon as he's hit he'll fall down and everyone will run away - leaving him completely unprotected."

The Chief of Staff was about to reply, when Price interrupted, "Wait! There's movement on the roof of the adjacent building. I saw a brief flash on infrared. There's something on the far side of the pitched roof."

"You sure it's not an animal. Maybe a cat?"

"Not unless they've started carrying guns," Price joked whilst staring intently through the gun sight - seeing another brief glimpse of a figure a few seconds later.

"It's him," Price reported. "He keeps sticking his head up. I suspect he's trying to figure out if there really is someone waiting for him. "

"Will he see you?"

"Unlikely. The suppressor is covered and the windows in this apartment are the usual SIS standard. They've been treated to absorb any attempts to scan from the outside. He'll need far more sophisticated equipment than he's got access to right now, if he wants to see me inside."

"Maybe there's a roof entrance."

Price was about to add that the roof was a poor choice because Slavic Stepka would have to jump across the gap between the buildings and break in via a skylight, in the process making himself an easy target.

However, before he could, a flash of red next to him made him, rather uncharacteristically, jump.

In an instant, Price let go of the MP5 and swung around to see if anyone had sneaked in to the room behind him - his pistol in his hand - his heart racing.

It was pitch black. He couldn't even make out the door and determine if it was open.

The silence made it even worse. The only thing he could hear was his own breathing - which for some reason now seemed to be even louder than normal.

Price realised he would be an easy target if he stayed still. So, risking running in to a potential intruder, he dived across the room to the wall next to the door, slamming his body against the woodwork as he turned again, feeling his heart beating even faster, as he stared in to the darkness and swept his gun left and right whilst reaching back with his right hand to check the lock.

The door appeared to be undisturbed.

Price unclipped the monocular from his belt and switched it to infrared. Then, he scanned the room to be certain that he was alone.

In his earpiece Price heard, "Gamma four-two-four? Gamma four-two-four are you there?"

Price ignored the Chief of Staff as he swept the room again to be doubly sure. Then, after a few moments of silence, satisfied that he was alone, he returned to his position by the window, noticeably shaken.

Price didn't like surprises. He knew that was how many of his friends and colleagues over the years had lost their lives.

"This is Gamma-four-two-four. It's OK Sir, I thought I had an intruder. All clear here."

Suddenly, there it was again. A red flash.

This time, however, Price wasn't taken by surprise and managed to get a better look at it.

"This is Gamma four-two-four. We may have a small problem," he announced. "There would appear to be a sniper trained on me. I keep seeing a laser flash."

"Any idea who it is?"

"It's probably his guardian angel. That biker I suspect. The same assassin that scared the crap out of the family."

He was about to continue speaking when he saw Slavic Stepka reappear on the rooftop. He was crouched down and presumably about to make the leap across the gap to the hotel.

"Gamma four-two-four, are you able to get a location on the sniper? If so, we can alert local forces to deal with it."

"Wait," Price replied - almost as a whisper, as his focus had changed. "Target is on the rooftop. He's quite well hidden, but in sight."

Slowing his breathing, Price relaxed to steady his hands and took aim - noting that the infrared signal had suddenly deteriorated.

Price glanced down at the gun, quickly checking the sight in case that was the problem. But it appeared to be functioning normally.

Then he realised what had happened.

Slavic Stepka had waited until the last second before wrapping himself in thick clothing - including using some kind of protective helmet.

And it had worked. His infrared signature was barely discernible.

Realising this pretty much ruled out a head shot, Price aimed at the body. Then he gripped the gun firmly with one hand, and with the other he gently squeezed the trigger.

The recoil and thud from the suppressor signalled that the bullet was on its way - a fraction of a second later striking his target, causing him to fall backwards.

"Strike. But he's wearing body armour," Price stated, as Slavic Stepka slowly crawled back in to position on the roof.

Price switched his gun to fully automatic and pulled the trigger again, firing a dozen or more bullets in a matter of seconds, just as a loud bang shattered part of the wall next to him.

Looking around, he could see the red laser searching for a target as the sniper repeatedly fired, smashing the window frame - the bullets striking the walls and ricocheting around the room.

"The sniper is enjoying himself. Please advise the local team that this apartment will require redecorating."

Price moved to one side so that he had more cover from the window frame and opened fire again.

His bullets slammed in to Slavic Stepka's body armour.

Price knew that body armour saved lives. However, he also knew that it could only take so much abuse. And, each strike would most definitely hurt.

They wouldn't necessarily be fatal - but he knew that Slavic Stepka would be feeling a great deal of pain, as he watched him slide down the pitched roof of the building and attempt to break-in via a window.

"This is my chance," Price thought - noting that the streetlight provided just the illumination he needed.

Switching his sight to its starlight setting, Price opened fire - missing by the smallest fraction of a second, as Slavic Stepka smashed through a window.

Undeterred, Price switched the sight back to infrared and increased the magnification so that he could clearly see Slavic Stepka wounded on the ground.

Price took aim again - thinking, "This time it's the kill shot."

But it wasn't to be.

A flash in the corner of his eye caught his attention and made him leap backwards - grabbing his rucksack and gun as he flung himself out of the room - using all of his bodyweight to smash the door down in the process.

"RPG," he shouted in to his headset, as the outside wall of the building exploded behind him.

The building's fire alarm was automatically activated, as hug crack appeared in the wall and dust filled the air.

Price leapt down the stairs - three and four at a time - to get himself to the ground floor. Then he ran around the side of the building and crouched down next to a wall.

Another RPG hit the apartment - this time devastating the frontage - causing part of the roof to collapse in to the road.

Price didn't care though. He just looked across the street to where Slavic Stepka had broken in to the building next to the hotel.

The window was clearly smashed to pieces on the fourth floor.

As a third RPG hit the building next to him, Price looked up the road - seeing a small figure clad in black turn to get on to a motorbike.

Price took aim, knowing that this would be close to the maximum range of the MP5. But he didn't care. It would be an instinctive shot - his favourite type. So, he aimed slightly high and a tiny fraction to the left, noting that the figure was moving. Then he fired four shots in quick succession - confident that all four hit their target, as he watched the figure in black fall to the ground and crawl away in to a dark corner behind a building.

"Strike on the sniper," he announced to the Chief of Staff, as he adjusted his grip - switching to the mini-grenade launcher attachment. Then, just as the figure in black tried to look around the side of the building, he fired a volley of grenades down the road.

He knew they would not reach their target. But that didn't matter. That wasn't their purpose. They were intended to surprise and suppress any attack whilst he sprinted across the road - blasting down the front door of the building where Slavic Stepka was now hiding.

Bursting through the door, Price stepped to one side and out of the light that shone in from the road, so that he would be less visible. Then he carefully looked around the dark room.

His first reaction was, "This is a total mess," followed by, "OK, I get it. it's being refurbished."

In front of him and to the left, there was a grand old wooden staircase that wound its way up the building.

The remainder of the room, however, appeared to be a combination of workman's tools, paint containers and decorating materials that were spread around in a seemingly random fashion.

Loud steps from above made Price run forward and sprint up the stairs as he reminded himself, "This is a five-story building. Four to go."

A gunshot narrowly missed his head, as Price flung himself to the side of the staircase - returning fire with his MP5 set on automatic, before running further up.

Another shot hit the stairs next to his feet. But Price was undeterred in his chase, as he again returned fire, running at full speed - adrenaline driving him forward.

Approaching the fifth story, Price knew that Slavic Stepka would have to hold his ground and make a stand. He'd have to defend himself or make a counter attack.

So, as he reached the top landing, Price slowed down and approached cautiously - seeing a body lying face down by a doorway.

He could clearly see that it wasn't Slavic Stepka, and was about to turn the body over to see who it was when a voice in his head screamed, "Stop! What are you doing!"

It was a memory from his SIS counter-intelligence training. A memory of the training where he had been taught how to inflict brutal injuries on the enemy and how to avoid having them being inflicted on himself.

Instead of touching the body, Price carefully walked around it. And sure enough, there it was - a hand-grenade with the pin removed - resting somewhat precariously under the left arm.

"You bastard," Price muttered to himself as he carefully retrieved the grenade, whilst keeping the lever pressed to prevent detonation.

Price glanced back at the staircase - thinking, "Well, they are already decorating. So why not?" as he tossed it down the stairwell.

The explosion three seconds later, sent shrapnel in all directions - narrowly missing Price who was crouched down next to a wall - his MP5 pointing at the doors on the other side of landing.

As he'd expected, Slavic Stepka opened the door to check that his trap had worked.

But it hadn't. It had failed and Price opened fire the instant he appeared.

Slavic Stepka fell back in to the room - slamming the door closed in the process.

Price knew that he had been wearing body armour, so, rather cruelly, he had aimed for the knees.

Slavic Stepka - his legs now broken and bleeding - used all his remaining strength to crawl to the window. He knew that if he stayed where he was, he only had seconds to live.

Price was well aware that he'd gained the advantage and fired a mini-grenade at the door - blowing it apart. Then, he ran forward bursting in to the room, just as Slavic Stepka dived out of the window head first - crashing through the glass and down in to a tarpaulin canopy fixed to the second story of the building, which slowed his decent before smashing him in to the roof of a parked car.

Price leaned out of the window - eager to finally bring the chase to an end. But as soon as he looked down, automatic gun fire hit the walls around him.

Yet again, it was the figure in black - firing from street level with one arm, whilst dragging Slavic Stepka in to the back of a police van parked at the side of the road.

Price leapt back from the window, turned and sprinted down what remained of the building's grand old staircase - running out in to the road just as the van drove away.

He desperately wanted to open fire - but there were quite a few civilians around.

Despite the early hour, people had started to emerge from all directions - he assumed, as a result of hearing all the explosions and gunfire.

Suddenly the Chief of Staff spoke in to Price's earpiece, "We have you on CCTV. Take the shot at the driver Gamma-four-two-four."

"Negative, there are too many people."

"Target the van then. Take the shot. You may be able to stop it. That is an order."

Price raised his weapon and looked through the MP5's telescopic sight.

Sure enough, the driver was clearly visible through the back window of the van. And rather oddly, appeared to have removed the protective helmet that had previously prevented identification.

For a brief second, as Price zoomed the MP5's sight in, he was able to see the driver's face in the van's rear-view mirror.

By pure chance, it happened just as the driver was looking in the mirror.

For a fleeting second, it almost felt like they had made eye contact.

"Take the shot!" the Chief of Staff shouted again.

Price froze - his only thought being, "What?"

Another shout from the Chief of Staff snapped Price back in to action.

He estimated he had maybe ten or fifteen seconds before the van would be out or range. So, he aimed and fired - hitting the passenger side of the back door of the van.

Adjusting his aim, Price fired again - taking out the rear wheels of the van, which veered violently across the road as the driver struggled to maintain control.

"That's your mistake," Price thought, as he had a brief glimpse of one of the front wheels.

He fired a short burst of bullets - shredding the tyre in an instant and making the driver lose all control of the vehicle, which now made a violent ninety-degree turn to the right before rolling on to its side.

"Yes! Nice shot," the Chief of Staff yelled in his ear. "Get after them!"

But Price new better, as he sprinted at full speed down the road.

He'd briefly had a perfect shot at the driver, but had elected to hit the passenger side of the vehicle instead. And only he knew why.

"Police incoming," the Chief of Staff reported - closely followed by, "You may have less welcoming company as well."

"Who?"

"Looks like Russia putting down a rogue agent. GCHQ are reporting that their communications have gone what they described as, totally nuts. Basically, they have a large team on their way and you don't want to meet them."

"Roger that," Price replied as he sprinted to the front of the upturned van and pointed his MP5 through the smashed windscreen.

"Good morning," he said.

Mary was not pleased to see him and gave a sarcastic reply as she struggled to undo her seatbelt.

"This really wasn't very helpful you know."

Looking to the back of the van, Price could see that Slavic Stepka was barely conscious.

The multiple gunshot wounds in his legs were bleeding profusely and his left arm was clearly broken - Price presumed from the fall. It also looked like the shot to the rear passenger door of the van had struck the right side of his body.

"Can I kill him?"

"No!" Mary shouted. "I need to speak to him."

"Why?"

Mary sighed, "Because I need to find out what he told everyone. Why else do you think I kept him alive, dumb arse!"

Price nodded as he said, "I can see the logic in that. So, go and ask him some questions. And be quick!"

"Yes darling, I will. But as you can see, I'm trapped in this damned seatbelt. Give me your knife, would you? I'll have to cut it, it's got jammed."

"Sure," Price replied, as he leaned in to the window and smashed his left fist in to Mary's face - striking the cheek bone, just to the right of her nose and below her left eye.

He knew it would cause a black-eye and could see that he'd cut her lip as well as making her nose bleed. But, he also knew she would fully recover after a few days of pain - so he wasn't concerned.

Mary, despite her stunningly beautiful appearance, was extremely tough. She immediately stopped struggling with the seat belt and just looked back at Price as the blood streamed out of her nose - evidently unconcerned as it ran down over her cracked lip and dripped on to her clothes.

Before Price could speak, a quizzical expression appeared on her face. Then she said, "I guess that makes us a matching pair. What the fuck happened to your face?"

"I got in to a fight last night."

"Oh, was it you who lit up that guy last night? It was in the news. I'm proud of you darling. I didn't think you could be that cruel."

"Did you send him?"

"Yes. But I did tell them not to be seen - and definitely not to go near you."

"Why?"

"I do happen to love you darling."

"Yeah right. I'm tempted to hit you again."

Mary laughed, "Please go ahead. I doubt it will make much difference. I've only got so much blood!"

Before Price could reply, his earpiece came to life as the Chief of Staff spoke.

"We've lost sight of you. The police have closed down the CCTV. Communication is becoming intermittent as well."

Suddenly, Price heard gunfire. So, he stepped back and looked around the side of the van - seeing what appeared to be a full-scale gun fight taking place between the police and, what he presumed were, Russian assassins out to get Slavic Stepka.

Looking back in to the van, he said, "We need to move, it's getting nasty out here."

Mary, despite the blood gushing from her nose, just pointed at the seat belt. So, Price leaned in again - this time handing her the knife that had been strapped to his leg.

Mary cut the seat belt and climbed in to the back of the van.

Looking back at Price, she paused for a second before asking, "How long have we got?"

Price stepped back and looked around the side of the van again - horrified by what he was seeing. The road resembled a war zone and the police appeared to be losing. They were armed with pistols - whereas the Russians had arrived with sub machine guns.

Price knew the police would have called for support. But

he also knew that could take a few minutes. When it did arrive, however, it would mean the Russians would need to retreat - probably in their direction.

So, he said, "Maybe two or three minutes at the most. The police back-up will bring everything to a close."

Mary shouted, "OK," so as to be heard above the gunfire. Then she turned to Slavic Stepka.

She slapped his face hard to get his attention, then grabbed his right hand and used Price's knife to cut the little finger off.

Slavic Stepka cried out in pain as Mary proceeded to remove the finger next to it, equally brutally. A single stab and slicing motion.

For a second, he appeared to stare at her - the hatred clear in his eyes.

"What did you tell them?" Mary asked - her voice calm and composed.

Slavic Stepka gave a fake angry laugh as he spat out the words, "Fuck you bitch. You're dead already!"

Mary raised her right knee and then slammed it down on Slavic Stepka's chest - her full weight bearing down on him as she plunged the knife in to his shoulder - jamming it under the bone and deep in to his muscle.

Slavic Stepka cried out and started shaking. Mary had deliberately pierced a nerve - one of the most painful experiences possible.

Mary's expression was totally emotionless as she looked in to his eyes. Then she began to rotate the knife, to make the pain even more unbearable.

"What did you tell them?"

Slavic Stepka, as tough as he was, couldn't take that degree of pain and began to lose consciousness as he muttered something incoherently.

Mary knew she didn't have much time though. So, she grabbed the knife with both hands and twisted it violently, eliciting another shriek of agony, as Slavic Stepka's eyes opened wide in sheer terror.

Mary looked down at him and calmly repeated the same question again. "What did you tell them?"

Slavic Stepka coughed - a cough that spat blood into Mary's face, as he started to speak - slurring his words.

"I told them everything. And I mean everything. How you blackmailed me. How you used my brother. All the guns. Alexei. Everything. You can kill me but they will get you, you bitch."

Mary grabbed at the knife and pulled it out of his shoulder, briefly creating even more pain.

Then with a complete lack of concern, she used his own clothes to wipe the blood off the knife before climbing back in to the front of the van and out through the gap where the windscreen had once been.

"Can I kill him now?" Price asked, sarcastically.

Returning his knife, Mary smiled, "Yes. You may."

Price sighed, "At last," and raised his gun, just as Slavic Stepka managed to lift his head up and look forward. Then, with what appeared to be his final breath, he muttered, "Wait, I spared your."

Two thuds from Price's MP5 created holes in Slavic Stepka's head, mid-way between the eyes.

He fell backwards on to the floor of the van, unable to finish the sentence.

Mary, glanced around the side of the van then looked back at Price.

"Darling, we should go. They're coming this way and I must say, they really don't look very happy."

Price shouldered the MP5, tightened the straps on his rucksack, and said, "Follow me," as he led Mary to a side street - narrowly escaping bullets that ricocheted off the stone wall of a building next to them.

What started as a light jog, very quickly became a fully-fledged sprint when more bullets began to get closer and closer - bouncing off the cobbled stone road surface and walls of buildings.

"I'm glad they're not very good shots," Mary shouted, as they ran around a corner in to another street - zig-zagging through the small lanes in an attempt to get away.

"There," Price shouted - pointing at a churchyard with a solid stone wall. "We can take a few out as they come around the corner."

Catching their breath, they crouched down side by side, each with their MP5 submachine gun pointing through a gap in the ancient stone work of the wall.

In front of them was a T-junction - a quiet lane that ran from left to right. And directly ahead, the end of a smaller road that had just been their escape route.

For a brief moment, there was almost total silence. The only sound being the tweets of birds in the trees.

Price said, "You'd think they would be pleased. We saved them the trouble of shooting Slavic Stepka."

Mary gave Price a brief glance before replying, "I don't think they were only after him darling."

"Oh. Is there something I should know?"

Mary laughed, "Yes darling. There's a lot. I think I may have been a very naughty girl."

Price was focused on the road ahead, but allowed himself to briefly glimpse Mary's face as he joked, "I'll spank you later!"

"Promises, promises!"

Price was about to reply when he saw a group of six armed men reach the end of the road directly across from them and stop. They were clearly trying to figure out which way Price and Mary had run.

"Three each?" Mary whispered.

"You're certain we can't talk them out of this?"

"Certain darling."

"OK, they're about to spread out. On three?"

"OK."

"Three!"

A short burst from each of their MP5's left the six men on

the ground, dead.

Mary looked across to Price, "Make sure?"

Price nodded and they both carefully took aim placing a single shot in to the head of each man.

Price turned to Mary as he said, "It was very clever of you to get him to use Grandma for the passport - that made sure I wouldn't kill him whilst he was in the UK."

Mary nodded in agreement. "I introduced them a while back. It made sense because it also meant I could track him."

"How?"

"She put a tracker chip in the passport. Only enough power to last a couple of days - but long enough to make sure I could be where I needed to be to keep that bastard alive until I could question him."

"He said he told them everything. Precisely what is the everything he told them?"

Mary briefly made eye contact as she said, "It will take some time to explain. But you like the passport idea, right? I was proud of that."

Price appreciated the ingenuity as he reached back in to his rucksack and retrieved a spare magazine to reload his weapon. Then, thinking back to their escape from the Russians, he said, "There were way more than six. What happened to the rest of them?"

Mary suddenly looked extremely worried.

"I don't know. I lost track of them as we ran for our lives. Damnit, we need to find some transport."

"We need to get out of here."

As if deliberately designed to make their predicament even worse, two black 4x4's arrived at the road in front of them - screeching to a halt next to the bodies.

Mary looked at Price and nodded towards the church, then they both silently crawled away, only standing and sprinting once they were completely out of view.

"I think we've lost them," Price declared. "At least, we have for the moment. Let's ditch the weapons and get the hell out of here."

"I need to go and search Stekpa's belongings."

"What? Why?"

"Darling, when I followed him here he had a rucksack, which he left behind when he came to the hotel. I know he always made notes of everything because he didn't have a very good memory. I need to destroy the notebook. If someone else finds it, it could potentially cause me a huge problem."

Price sighed, "You're not making this easy, are you? Why didn't you take it off him when you followed him? You know it's best to deal with things like that before the shooting starts!"

"I'm sorry, but I couldn't. He drove to an old factory where he left the rucksack. He was in and out so fast, I didn't get a chance to intercept him. And I couldn't search for it whilst he was going to the hotel, because I had to follow him and stop you killing him."

"You could have just phoned me and told me not to shoot him."

"If I'd have done that, would you have listened?"

Staring in to Mary's eyes, Price said, "Yeah, I would. If you'd said it mattered, I would have. And let me ask you, if the situation was reversed, would you do that for me?"

Mary laughed, "Of course. That's easy."

Then, after a pause, she added, "Sorry. I should have told you that I was wearing a bulletproof vest as we went to leave the cottage. It all happened so quickly."

Price nodded. "Apology accepted. Never to be discussed again. So where is this place?"

"It's a very old abandoned factory about five miles out of town."

"I guess we could hike it, Price pondered. "How busy are the roads between here and there?"

"Too busy darling. We need transport."

"OK, let's find a car. Something old - the new ones are almost impossible to steal."

Unfortunately, their conversation had caused them to lose focus. They'd failed to take precautions as they rounded a corner - only to be faced with three police cars.

Both Mary and Price stopped dead as she said, "Back up slowly. Maybe they're not very observant."

But it was too late - the sirens switched on as they turned and ran back down the lane towards the rear of the churchyard. Without so much as another word, they'd read each other's mind, as the police screeched around the corner, only to be faced with the two 4x4's full of armed men.

Rather than face another fight, the 4x4's took off at speed, leaving the bodies behind.

Two police cars set off after them, leaving the third one with three police officers inside, to track down Price and Mary.

As the three officers got out of the car, they all had their guns raised - pointing forward.

"This is a problem," remarked Mary. "It's rule number one. You don't shoot people who are basically on your own side."

"It is a challenge," Price agreed. "However, I will defend myself and they will get shot if they push their luck!"

Mary adjusted her position to get a better view from behind the churchyard wall - not realising that the piece of turf she was kneeling on was not that solid. Consequently, as she moved, it moved as well and caused her to slip - in the process causing her MP5 to hit a metal upright in the wall.

The loud clanging sound broke the silence and clearly identified where they were hiding.

Mary looked at Price, recognizing the mistake.

"Oops."

Price just smiled - fully aware that it could easily have been him who made exactly the same mistake.

Then he said, "OK, let's assess this. We have three officers. One is clearly senior, whilst the other two appear to be quite junior - a male and a female."

"We can't kill them," Mary declared. "We both know

that's a step too far."

"Hopefully not," Price conceded. "How about, I distract them and you take their car. I'll meet you at the factory."

"That's a deal," Mary agreed, as she carefully crawled to her right to take advantage of the curvature of the wall and bring her slightly closer to the police car.

Price waited for her to get in position, then he jumped to his feet and sprinted across the road, past the dead bodies and, fired a mini-grenade at a door, blasting his way in to an office block.

He heard the police officers shouting and shortly after a bullet ricocheted off a wall a few yards away.

But Price wasn't worried.

He knew that the first instinct of all decent police officers would not be to fire their weapon - outside of the USA that is, where shooting as many people as possible appears to be the default reaction to pretty much everything, of course.

As Price watched the police car drive away, he almost laughed - whilst making a note of the call sign printed on the side, "whisky echo x-ray five seven one."

For her part, Mary had realised that the car was a hybrid, and had switched it to electric motors only. She had driven away in almost total silence, whilst thinking, "They'll be really confused when they turn around."

Taking cover in the building, Price thought he could just slip away unseen - maybe exiting via a rear door. However, it wasn't that easy. It turned out that the local police had a genuine hero in their mix.

The young female officer ran forward, shouting that Price should surrender, whilst firing her gun.

Price stepped slightly further back in to the safety of the building, whilst also noting that the officer had advanced nearly twenty meters and was now hiding behind a parked car.

The officer ran forward again a few seconds later. But this time he was expecting her.

Price knew he had to be careful. After all, as Mary had said, they were on the same side. So, he took time to aim, before firing a single shot to the right thy.

The officer stumbled and fell down. But to her credit, despite being wounded, she carried on firing and even reloaded whilst Price looked on in total amazement.

Then, realizing it had been only a glancing blow, the officer slowly rose to her feet with the clear intention to advance even further.

Price couldn't believe what he was seeing. The officer was now in the middle of the road with no cover, and yet seemed to want to continue attacking.

As she ran forward, Price fired again. It was another shot with pinpoint accuracy - this time to the officer's left thy. Another flesh wound that would cause no lasting injuries, but again caused the officer to stumble and fall down.

The officer rolled over on the ground in pain. Then, to Price's astonishment, the older, clearly more senior officer walked out in to the open with his hands in the air.

Price smiled. He respected both the bravery and the wisdom. He knew this was the action of an individual who had also recognized that Price didn't want to kill a police officer.

Sure enough, as the older gentleman recovered his junior colleague, Price took the opportunity to escape via the rear of the building.

Running as fast as he could, Price darted down the old lanes as if his life depended on it.

Then, as he ran away from the centre of the city, his earpiece suddenly sprang to life - the Chief of Staff's voice shouting, "Gamma-four-two-four are you there?"

"Here Sir."

"Status?"

"Target is dead."

"Well done my friend. Well done. Get yourself to the local office and come home."

"Negative Sir. Sorry, but I need to help a friend."

"Gamma-four-two-four you have your orders."

"If I recall Sir, I'm on holiday and this trip never took place. So, if it's OK with you, I think I will go and sit on a beach."

"With your MP5?"

"We're best buddies. We go way back."

There was a pause. Then the Chief of Staff said, "The friend. Female by any chance?"

"Yes."

"Not dead after all."

"No Sir."

"You need to remember who your real friends are and where your loyalties belong Price."

"That was uncalled for. That has never changed. But I will not watch a friend be killed by a bunch of criminals - that itself, is a crime."

The Chief of Staff smiled in agreement - pleased at Price's emotional response which just validated his loyalty. Then he said, "Don't get yourself killed in the process."

"No shit Sir! See you next week."

There was another pause, then the Chief of Staff said, "Let me know if you need some back up."

Price hesitated, then asked, "Can you track and trace police vehicle whisky echo x-ray five seven one?"

The Chief of Staff replied immediately, "Yes, that's easy - we can see all the transponders. Why?"

"She's in that one."

"You need to find some transport. Whisky echo x-ray five seven one is parked at an old disused factory on the outskirts of the city. At least it was when it last sent a signal. Someone's disabled the tracker by the looks of it. It's a few miles away. Find something fast, before she buggers off."

Price looked around, as he said, "Roger that."

There were plenty of cars - but they were all modern and almost certainly protected by advanced security systems.

Then, out of the corner of his eye, he noticed a small motorbike.

"That'll do," he thought as he pulled it off its stand, jammed one of the tools from his locking picking kit in to the hole where the key would normally go, and started the engine.

"I'm on my way," he announced, as the engine roared to life and he raced down the road - all the while receiving directions in his earpiece.

16. The Traitor

The factory building was vast. A huge remnant of the former soviet era.

A concrete structure with vertical lines that were, in some ways, reminiscent of the art deco stylings that had been prevalent back in the nineteen twenties and thirties.

Whilst in a decaying state of repair, it towered over the surrounding area - a largely deserted wasteland that presumably would have once thrived with activity. Now, however, it was just a place of cracked concrete and broken outbuildings, where shrubs and weeds were re-establishing themselves - over time returning the land to nature.

Price could see the police car from a distance. It was parked near the main entrance and had been left with the doors wide open.

"This is Gamma four-two-four, I am arriving at the factory and can see the police vehicle."

There was no reply, so Price tried again, "This is Gamma four-two-four, do you read me?"

After a few seconds, he heard the Chief of Staff's voice, somewhat muted by extremely poor sound quality.

"We're losing your signal Gamma four-two-four. The reception in that location is really poor. What's your status?"

"I can see the car. It's unoccupied. I'll head in to the

building."

"Understood Gamma four-two-four. However, we are losing your signal. You're on your own. Good luck."

"Roger that. Over and out."

Part of Price was relieved, as he removed the headset and placed it in his pocket.

He hated having wearing communication devices that disturbed his natural senses.

Despite what everyone said, he was sure they affected his performance during exercises and on operations - particularly, when he was attempting a discrete entry in to a building - something he was about to attempt once again.

He hoped that the building would be empty - aside from Mary. However, experience had taught him that it was always best to assume the worst.

Glancing down at his mobile phone, Price looked at a map of the building that the Chief of Staff had sent him during the short drive.

The building was a maze of corridors and hundreds of rooms over ten stories.

The map provided a recommended entry - a service door at the rear of the building that wasn't overlooked by any windows. An access point that was inevitably risky - but in their judgement, as safe as possible.

Price parked the bike out of sight of the main road and approached the wooden service door. It had one large lock that he opened with ease.

Inside, he walked through a small room, out through another door and in to a large atrium that spanned the height of the building.

Looking around, Price knew the sun would be lighting up the sky in the next hour or so. It was critical that he found Mary and they get the hell out of there, fast.

So, he switched the gun sight on the MP5 to its UV setting. Unlike the infrared setting that only picked up body heat - and was, therefore, useless when trying to detect people through concrete - the high-intensity short-wave ultra-violet beam the sight produced, was able to penetrate relatively thin walls and give him a small advantage.

Whilst he had no idea where Mary would be, Price was fairly certain it would be around the perimeter - most likely on the north side of the building, as that was the direction of the main road and provided a good view of anyone else arriving.

Price also thought, "It's probably on a medium-to-high floor, because that's what I would do."

He studied the map one last time before pocketing the phone - keeping a mental image in his head - a skill he'd been taught during SIS training many years before. Then, with the gun sight to his eye, Price gradually made his way up a flight of stairs to the next level - all the while scanning for any sign of life.

It was eerily quiet, aside from the occasional rat scurrying down a corridor or a bird flying through the broken roof.

He couldn't help thinking that it was a strange place for Slavic Stepka to have picked.

"Or is this just another trap?" he wondered. "Am I about to walk around a corner and find myself faced with a dozen armed men? Or just get shot in the back before I can even react?"

On reaching the fourth floor, Price stopped dead in his tracks, as he stared through the gun sight - identifying two blue outlines in a room ahead of him.

Switching the sight to maximum intensity, he could clearly see that there were two people inside the room. Assuming one of them was Mary, it was clear that she had company. Although, whilst one appeared to be crouched in a corner smoking a cigarette, the other appeared to be hanging upside down from the ceiling.

For a brief moment, Price regretted letting Mary drive to the factory on her own. He'd lost her once, only to find her alive. He couldn't help feeling that this time her luck had run out.

The walls were too thick for him to be able to make out any features. So, with that in mind, he decided that an explosive entry was the safest way to proceed.

Reaching in to his rucksack, Price retrieved some plastic explosive and a stun grenade - the legendary flash-bang, named after its effect - a bright flash followed by a loud bang that disorientates any normal person.

"Not that I ever meet anyone who could be described as normal whilst doing this job," Price reminded himself.

Being careful not to be heard, he placed the plastic explosive around the frame of the door, inserted a remote-controlled detonator and stood well back.

A quick glance through the gun sight confirmed that the

two figures had not moved.

"This is it," he thought, as he squeezed the trigger on the remote control - his MP5 raised and ready to fire, just in case it did not work as expected.

The explosion was far larger than Price had intended, as it removed part of the wall as well. But he didn't hesitate. He'd trained for this hundreds of times and immediately threw in the flash-bang, which exploded as he burst in to the room.

In a fraction of a second, he identified Mary siting in the corner - an unknown figure, hanging upside down from the ceiling.

"It's just me Price. He's dead. Save the bullets," Mary's calm voice reassured him. "I'm going to switch the lights back on now. OK?"

Price didn't immediately answer. He scanned the large room through the gun sight - wanting to be sure they really were alone.

Then Mary said, "Well, I'm switching on the lights anyway, so if you don't want to be blinded, I suggest you stop looking through the gun sight."

With a lamp lighting the room, Price walked around the body that was hanging upside down.

It was clear that the man had been repeatedly tortured in the most brutal way possible - he presumed by Mary.

There was blood everywhere on the body and multiple fingers missing - not to mention the large patch of blood that was still dripping from the man's groin.

Price didn't even want to imagine what cruelty Mary had inflicted to that part of his body - it didn't bare thinking about.

"Nice explosive entry by the way," Mary remarked, almost casually. "If I were normal, it would have scared the life out of me."

"Lucky you're not then," Price replied.

"Yes. I guess so."

"Who was he?" Price asked, deliberately using the past tense to try and annoy Mary.

His attempt failed. Her blank, emotionless response said it all.

"I don't know."

"Did you manage to get him to speak?"

"No."

"You tortured him."

"Yes."

"And you got nothing?"

"Only screams and a lot of crying."

"Nothing useful?"

"No."

Price just shrugged his shoulders. "I guess it doesn't always work."

"No shit Sherlock!"

Price glanced down at Mary, noting some burnt paper on the floor next to her - he presumed the remains of Slavic Stepka's note book.

As he walked over to the window to check that they were still alone, he said, "I thought you'd given up smoking."

Mary flicked the cigarette away.

"You're right," she said. "I'm sorry, it is a filthy habit."

Price looked back in to the room.

"You owe me some answers. Starting with, why did Stepka want to kill you, why did Alexei want to kill you? And why did you want to kill Alexei?"

"Price, we don't have time for this."

"We have a few minutes I'm sure."

"We don't have time!"

Price pointed his MP5 directly at Mary's head, then said, "You have time. Answer now or sleep forever!"

Mary sighed.

"Stepka worked for me. I recruited him many years ago when I discovered he was messing with kids."

"You blackmailed him."

Mary's tone was almost defensive as she replied, "You'd have done the same Price."

"Oh absolutely. Don't get me wrong," he agreed. "I wasn't accusing you. He was fair game and you were doing your job. Please continue."

Mary gave a half-smile. She wasn't happy, but understood what Price meant. Then she said, "What are we like?"

"Ruthless. It's the job. Carry on or shall I pull the trigger?"

Mary paused - making eye contact to try and determine how real Price's threat was.

But she couldn't read him. For the first time since they had been a couple, she was struggling.

So, she simply said, "As you would expect, I used the information against him because, if that had got back to the Russians, they'd have killed him without so much as a second thought - as he knew.

But then he rebelled.

He didn't seem to care that I might tell his superiors that he was now a double-agent. So, I tried to meet him - to find out what was going on. I was thinking of asking him to kill Alexei who, by the way, was blackmailing me."

"Hold on, you're going too fast. Why did he rebel?"

"It turns out that the Russians discovered I was running him, so they tried to get him to set me up and kill me, in exchange for his freedom. He'd been in prison in the past for some truly awful things - not just messing with kids - other stuff. He was an awful human being.

Anyway, he failed to kill me and then his brother got killed in a bus accident in London. He must have thought it was some kind of conspiracy against him and he went kind of crazy."

"Did he know how his brother died?"

Mary looked at Price inquisitively.

"I heard it was an accident. A bus, right?"

Price nodded no as he said, "He was shot, whilst carrying out a mugging. He skidded under the bus, because he had a bullet in his back."

"That never made the news."

"Well, that's because I'm not supposed to use my gun in London."

"In that case, maybe he did know it was MI6 that killed his brother. Anyway, whatever he was thinking, he went crazy and was most definitely trying to kill me."

"What happened to Alexei? I thought he worked for you?"

"He did initially. But more recently it ended up being the other way around. Alexei discovered that, amongst other things, I was running Stepka. That was why I used Stepka and his brother to kill Vitaly Isaev in London."

Price was shocked, "Hang on a minute. You killed Vitaly?"

"Yes, I was ordered to by Alexei, otherwise he was going to hand over evidence of my other activities to my superiors. I had no choice."

"But why Vitaly?"

"Darling you and I both know Vitaly was working for MI6."

Price smiled, "Yes I know that, but how did Alexei know? Don't tell me you have more people in my service? That would be very depressing."

Mary laughed. "You know something Price. It was one of those things. It was random. That Italian restaurant that Stepka attacked, looking for me? Well I was there many months ago meeting Chinese officials from our London office. It was a quiet place to also meet Vitaly. We planned to try and turn him - to get him working for us.

In preparation for that, we put him under very close surveillance - for quite a long time I might add. And he made a mistake. He gave himself away.

Your people were very careful - very careful indeed. But, he was ex-army. His attitude was to confront - to face things head-on. So, on one occasion after we'd been tracking him - and lost him I have to admit - he made a mobile phone call to his wife, whilst on the way home from an MI6 meeting.

And before you say it, yes, he had taken it with him to a meeting with one of your people, which I'm sure he'd been told not to do. But he did. We listened in, he said something to his wife and in that second his cover was blown."

Price was stunned, "Wow!"

"Yes, I was quite surprised as well. Darling, don't be upset. It was him not your service. However, you may be slightly surprised when I tell that I tried to use that information to escape Alexei's attention."

"But that didn't work."

"No. He was a bastard. I offered it to him thinking that identifying a double-agent would make him look good and get him off my back. Instead, he decided that the way to make himself look good was to instruct me to get rid of Vitaly. That's how all this started."

"But why a nerve agent? That's just evil."

"Oh, that was someone's ego. They wanted to send a message. I was horrified at the idea. But I wasn't exactly in control of the decisions as you can imagine."

"Is there any more nerve agent out there?"

"Not that I'm aware of."

"What went wrong?"

"Well, as I say, it would have been fine. Then it turns out that you killed Stepka's brother and he went crazy. Although, I think the stress of his past time in prison had been building inside him. So, his brother's death probably just tipped him over the edge.

Then, as far as I can tell, there was an investigation. They discovered that Alexei knew about me running Stepka and that he hadn't reported it. So, he was labelled a traitor along with Stepka."

"And you! Let's not forget there were three traitors in this mess. Alexei, Stepka and you!"

"Kind of you to remind me Price."

"That explains why you wanted Alexei dead."

"Yes. If you'd have got him, then I could have focused on Stepka."

"We intercepted a message the other day, along the lines of I've done as you asked. Was that you?"

"Maybe. I did send one like that. But I suspect Stepka sent the same message back to his superiors after shooting us at the cottage.

He thought he'd succeeded in his task. I'm fairly sure the

message he sent was his last desperate attempt to get accepted back in to Russia."

"So, you were trying to kill both of them and Slavic was trying to kill both of you."

"Yes."

"They should never have let Stepka out of prison in the first place. That was poor judgement."

"You're right darling. He told me that the only reason they did was because they needed someone for what was effectively a suicide mission."

Price laughed, "And he survived it."

"Yes. Most unfortunate."

"Out of curiosity, which prison was Stepka in?"

"Well he spent some time in a brutal place called Black Eagle."

"That is bad," Price agreed.

"Yes, but then he went to a place that's even worse. Although, I would argue it was the right place for someone as sick as him. Black Dolphin. Have you heard of it?"

"I have. I've been there actually."

Somewhat surprised, Mary said, "You've been there?"

"We had an informant who got locked up there. I guess the stress must have got to him. He lost the plot and went on a killing spree - he was totally out of control."

"If he was that bad, why did you save him?"

Before Price could reply, Mary added, "And anyway, that's not possible. Nobody has ever escaped from Black Dolphin. What happened?"

"A team of us dropped in nearby and hacked in to their system."

"Darling, their prison systems are not accessible from the outside."

Price nodded, "I know the prison system isn't. But in the event of a fire, they do automatically alert the fire service. So, we hacked the fire system and set the fire alarm off instead."

"Then what?"

"Quite sensibly, under heavy guard, they moved all the prisoners out in to the yard whilst they searched for the fire - at which point I shot him in the head with a sniper's rifle from just over half a mile away."

"That's a very good shot. As I understand it, the yard is actually a cage."

"It is," replied Price. "There are bars overhead as well. I was quite pleased with the shot. Unlike the guards at Black Dolphin, who went completely nuts when his head exploded and he dropped to the ground."

Mary laughed. "They should be grateful. The record still stands. Nobody has ever escaped from Black Dolphin."

"I would argue it was an escape of sorts. Definitely for us, because we were convinced he'd leak information before long."

Mary didn't reply. However, after a short pause Price

asked, "What other things?"

"What do you mean?"

"You said you were running Stepka amongst other things. What other things were you up to? All this stuff about you being a very naughty girl. None of what you've just described is that bad in our business. I get that, in normal life it's horrific - but not for us. So, what's going on?"

"Oh, I had a small side business. You see, I was bored so I err, smuggled some arms on the side."

"So, you were the brains behind Stepka's smuggling. I heard about that."

Mary just shrugged her shoulders as she said, "Sorry."

"Well it's over now."

"If only life was that simple darling. His last message was extremely unfortunate as it gave me away."

"What are you saying?"

"It was in his notes," Mary replied - pointing to the burnt remnants next to her. He really did tell them everything. And not just to the Russians. He told everyone everything."

"Well it stops here. As I said, it's over," Price insisted.

"It is darling, but not in the way you mean. The whole world is about to come crashing down. When he admitted that I was the agent running him, they found everything. So, this really is the end for me."

Price sighed, "Mary, as a famous person once said. This is not the end. It's not even the beginning of the end. It may, however, be the end of the beginning."

There was a pause as they stared at each other.

Mary eventually breaking the silence with, "Very poetic Price, but."

She never got a chance to finish her sentence - the sound of screeching tyres made Price turn and look back out of the window.

Six unmarked black Range Rover 4x4's had pulled up and were blocking the road to the north.

As the doors opened, Price counted twenty armed men in what looked like special forces outfits, moving towards the building.

"Were you expected this?" he asked.

"Yes."

"How did they find us? Surely you deactivated the tracker on the police car when you arrived. In fact, I know you did."

"Yes, I did. But not immediately, as I needed you to find me darling."

"And anyway," Mary added as she held up a mobile phone, "Stepka left his mobile here. And the bastard left it switched on. He must have known I'd come here. So, he wanted to make sure other people could find us."

"Who are they?"

"I don't know darling. They could be Russian special forces, Slovakian special forces, Czech, Ukrainian, Georgian. Take your pick. I think I've managed to upset them all over the last twelve months."

Price laughed, "You've been very busy."

"I was bored. And you know what they say about the devil and idle hands."

"He's a bastard?"

"Something like that darling, yes."

Price didn't immediately reply. He continued to watch as half of the men spread out to cover the building's main exits, whilst the rest smashed their way through the doors at the front.

Then he remarked, "They don't look like they're after an autograph."

"No. I suspect they want to fuck me darling. And not necessarily in a good way."

Price smiled as he walked to the door. Then looking back, he said, "There are many ways out of this is a grand old building. Way more than a couple of dozen men can cover. Follow me."

"It's over darling - accept it."

"Mary, it's not over until the fat lady sings."

Mary laughed. "What's got in to you today? That's another famous quote. An opera reference if I'm not mistaken."

Price paused. "D'you know, I'm not entirely sure where that phrase originated. Shall we stop for a while and google it?"

Still laughing, Mary picked up her MP5, stood up and

walked to Price's side. Then looping her arm through his, she kissed him on the cheek and whispered, "Maybe later?"

"You're probably right. Let's go."

As they walked out in to the hallway, both Price and Mary relied on their military training - silently sprinting towards the south and rear of the building, whilst using their gun sights to scan the rooms ahead of signs of life.

Three floors below, they could hear shouting and loud bangs, as the armed assailants searched the building.

"We need transport," whispered Mary, as they slowly made their way down a fire exit to the rear of the building.

"I have a motorbike," Price replied.

"Fantastic. A bike will do nicely."

"It's only 125cc."

Mary stopped and looked at Price - briefly lowering her weapon.

"That's just embarrassing."

"Hey, I'm not the one that seems to have pissed off half of the world. Why are they so angry with you by the way? You smuggled arms for them. It's not particularly ethical, but it's not that bad."

"It is actually," Mary remarked. "Because, quite a few of the arms didn't actually work. I got them on the black market. They were the shipments that failed quality control, so I got them really cheaply."

"But charged the full amount I assume?"

"Of course. Otherwise it would have been suspicious."

Price smiled, "I can see why that might cause a certain level of angst, shall we say. Were there many?"

"Thousands. Many thousands."

Price ignored the reply, as he looked down - holding his arm out to signal Mary to stop as well.

There were two men standing at the bottom of the stairs who, fortunately didn't appear to have seen them.

It was too late though - a shout from above was immediately followed by bullets raining down around them - ricocheting off the walls and handrail.

Price pointed to a door that would lead them off the fire escape.

"Second floor. West side fire exit," he said. "That's actually closer to the bike."

Mary looked up and down then said, "Wait. Fun first." Then she fired upwards, immediately before firing down at the two men below.

Both groups of men returned fire as Mary followed Price back through the door.

Price smiled. "Nicely done. Now they're firing at each other."

As they ran to the west side of the building and sprinted down the fire escape, they could still hear the guns firing.

It was only as the motorbike's engine roared in to life that the guns finally stopped - immediately followed by lots of shouting. And then, as they rode across rough ground, Price was sure he heard the 4x4's engines in the distance.

"Where are we headed," he asked as he changed gear, pushing the bike as hard as he dared.

Mary was way ahead of him - having already retrieved her mobile phone and viewed the map.

"There's a small airfield near here. Some kind of light aircraft training centre. How are your flying skills these days?"

"I'm a bit rusty actually," replied Price, as he pushed the bike's engine even harder whilst Mary glanced back.

"They're gaining," she said. "They're quite a way back, but I can see the dust as they cover the rough ground."

"We have no choice," said Price. "We have to keep going. Apart from my Smith and Wesson, I'm out of ammo."

"Me too," Mary commented. "The shots I fired back there were my last."

"There's a road ahead."

"Yes," Mary replied. "Hang a left. We'll dart through the village. I have an idea."

As the bike made the transition from rough ground to tarmac, Price nearly lost control - narrowly managing to keep it upright as he swerved to the left - before re-applying the throttle.

The sound of gunfire echoed around the narrow lanes of the village as Price cut every corner - desperate to prevent the gunmen getting a clean shot at them.

"Steps!" Mary shouted - tapping Price on his shoulder and pointing.

Price jumped on the brake, causing the wheels to screech as he turned, changed gear and dropped the clutch before screaming down some ancient stairs that linked the higher level of the village to its lower level, further down the hillside.

Ahead, he could see a small foot passage that, most importantly, was only around six feet wide.

"Where does that go?" he shouted - seeing the 4x4's bumping down the steps behind them - their suspension working overtime.

Mary glanced at her phone then shouted, "Take it!"

The 4x4's screeched to a halt at the end of the passage - the gunmen leaning out and firing to try and stop the bike, whilst the drivers tried to figure out an alternative route.

But they were too far away and Price swerved the bike around a corner, then another corner and finally out of sight.

In the distance behind them, they heard shouting and the 4x4 engines revving. But it didn't matter. They'd escaped.

At least, they had for now.

Ditching the bike at the side of a road, Price and Mary walked on to the airfield and straight in to what looked like an office.

It was only hours later that Mary realised why the staff had given them such a strange expression.

As she related to Price, "Imagine what we looked like. I had a black eye and a face covered in blood - and you had a black eye with scratches down the side of your face."

Despite the somewhat strange look, they were unable to strike what Price had hoped would have been an amicable deal. Consequently, what started as a perfectly civil conversation - asking to rent an aircraft - ended up with Price's Smith and Wesson dictating terms.

It wasn't how he preferred to do business - but as he increased the throttle and pulled back the stick, feeling the wheels get light as they lifted off the ground, he commented to Mary, "I'm sorry for them, but it was this or we get killed."

Mary looked out of the window - to her left and back down at the airfield.

"They're down there already," she said, as the 4x4's burst through the gates of the airfield with guns firing from the windows.

Price just looked across at Mary and smiled.

Then he said, "Which way?"

"West. And stay low, below a hundred and fifty feet. You're about to cross in to Austria. If we go in at altitude they'll be seriously pissed."

Price just nodded, as he eased back on the throttle and started to turn to the west - deliberately losing altitude in the process.

"We made it darling," Mary declared.

Price smiled.

However, it was to be a short-lived celebration. A few moments later, they heard the tell-tale sound of automatic weapons.

Price pushed the throttle forward, feeling the engine respond, increasing their speed to gain altitude again as Mary looked back out of the window.

"They've stolen a plane," she said. "Looks like there are four or five of them and they've got the doors open."

"Single engine like this?"

"Yes. Why?"

"Gives me an idea," replied Price, as he pulled back on the stick even further, feeling the nose lift.

Not expecting the sudden change in direction, Mary found herself being thrown to the rear of the aircraft - screaming in the process, as her head smashed against the fuselage.

"Ah! Shit! What the hell!" she shouted.

"You need to wear your seat belt," Price shouted back, with an element of humour in his voice.

"Son of a bitch!"

Mary slowly made her way back up to the front as Price continued to climb.

"What are you doing?"

Price glanced across at her.

"If they're full of people, they'll struggle to climb. We might be able to lose them on altitude alone."

Mary nodded agreement, before adding, "By the way, there's a parachute back there. Only one, but it might be useful."

Price turned his head to look at her. "Put it on would you. That gives me another idea."

"What?"

"Please, just put it on. Quickly!"

Mary nodded and ran to the back - strapped the parachute over her shoulders and sat down next to Price.

"Hold on to something," he said, as they suddenly heard bullets from the other plane, strike the bodywork.

Mary gripped the seat, as Price raised the aircraft's nose even further, taking it vertical and finally upside-down.

Mary looked at him - her expression asking if he knew what he was doing.

"They can't follow," he said. "They won't have the power with all those people inside."

Then, as their plane levelled out again, he said, "There," pointing forward. "We did a full three-sixty and now we're behind them. Get the door open and be ready to jump."

"What? Why?"

"I have a plan. Mary, do it please. And don't jump without me!"

Mary briefly touched his shoulder as she said, "Of course not darling. We leave together or not at all."

Then she ran back, gripped the handle by the door and

kicked it open - feeling the air rush in.

Glancing forward, seeing them closing on a collision course with the other plane at high speed, she shouted, "Price! What the fuck are you doing?"

She was too late though. Price had used their lighter weight and higher altitude to gain a huge amount of speed, before crashing in to the other aircraft - smashing the nose of their plane in to the area where the cabin compartment meets the wing.

The impact was so violent that Mary was thrown forward and in to the back of Price's seat, as he stood up.

"Ah! Fuck!" she screamed as her head hit the back of the seat and she heard her nose make a cracking sound.

Suddenly, the bracing that was holding the wing of the other aircraft in place, snapped with an almighty bang.

In an instant, the wing bent downwards, causing both planes to rotate sideways. Then, as the air resistance impacted the wings that were still intact on Price and Mary's plane, they started to tumble whilst plummeting towards the ground - locked together by the bent and broken bodywork.

Most of the occupants from the other plane found themselves thrown out of the smashed cockpit, falling to their inevitable death.

The two aircraft, meanwhile, now behaving as a single entity, rolled over and over again.

Price tried to reach Mary. But every time he moved, his legs were flipped over his head and he found himself crashing against the bodywork.

"Was this your plan?" Mary shouted, as she looked at Price, whilst clinging upside-down to a body panel.

"Yes," he shouted, as he finally managed to crawl towards her - only to be thrown against the ceiling again, as the body of the plane twisted and turned yet again.

"You're seriously telling me that you planned this shit?"

"Yes."

"Price, you're a dumbass!"

Price was going to reply, but at that moment he found himself being thrown on top of Mary, and quickly tried to grab one of the parachute straps - only to miss, as he was thrown upside-down again with his face being smashed against the floor.

"Did you just try and grab my breast?"

Price looked up at Mary - blood now gushing from his nose - and shouted. "No, I was grabbing for the strap."

Suddenly the plane twisted again, giving him another opportunity.

This time, as he grabbed at the strap he was able to make contact. So, with his other hand, he reached down and squeezed Mary's backside.

"What the fuck was that? There's no strap there."

"No. That was me grabbing your arse."

Mary sighed. "Men! Can we please get the fuck out of here?"

Price nodded, as they started to tumble their way towards the door, repeatedly banging their heads in to each other, before eventually flinging themselves through the gap and in to open space - narrowly missing a seat from the other aircraft that had become dislodged and zipped past them, missing their heads by only a few inches.

"Hold on tight," Mary shouted.

Price made eye contact and mouthed the words, "Pull the cord."

Mary didn't need to be told twice, and a second later the force of the parachute jolted their bodies - slowing their decent as they watched both aircraft spinning below them, finally crashing in to the ground, killing all the remaining occupants.

A few minutes later, they walked in to a quiet Austrian town - having crossed the border by accident - and headed straight for a car hire shop.

Mary said, "We need a holiday."

Price laughed, "We need to fix our faces first. We look like we've been in a fight."

"We have been in a fight darling. But putting that to one side for the moment, where shall we go?"

"UK?"

"Too close to your work."

"Far east?"

"Too close to my work."

"Africa?"

"We'll get killed or kidnapped."

"South America?"

"See Africa."

"Middle east?"

"Darling, that region is not exactly woman friendly."

"Good point. OK, then how about New Zealand?"

"Interesting, but too far away - and too many sheep!"

"Eastern Europe?"

"Too much vodka."

"Russia?"

"They want to kill me."

"Oh yeah - sorry."

"How about Scandinavia darling?"

Price smiled, "Yes, let's go there - lots of blonde girls!"

"Behave. Spain?"

"Actually, I really like Spain. Other options though?"

"Greece?"

"They're out of money."

"Italy?"

"Beautiful country - shame about the government."

Mary hesitated, then said, "OK, how about France?"

Price nodded in agreement as he said, "Yes. Paris is the

most wonderful place. We used to go there all the time."

"We had great sex in Paris."

"We had great sex in lots of places."

Mary laughed, "I'm glad you thought so!"

TO BE CONTINUED

Printed in Great Britain
by Amazon